Espresso and Evil

A Peridale Cafe MYSTERY

AGATHA FROST

pink tree
PUBLISHING

Copyright © Pink Tree Publishing Limited.

First published in print June 20th 2017

All characters and events in this publication, other than those clearly in the public domain, are fictitious and any resemblance to real persons, living or dead, is purely coincidental.

The moral right of the author has been asserted.

All rights reserved. This book or any portion thereof may not be reproduced or used in any manner whatsoever without the express written permission of the publisher except for the use of brief quotations in a book review.

For questions and comments about this book, please contact pinktreepublishing@gmail.com

www.pinktreepublishing.com
www.agathafrost.com

ISBN: 9781521522714
Imprint: Independently published

Other books in the Peridale Café Series

Pancakes and Corpses
Lemonade and Lies
Doughnuts and Deception
Chocolate Cake and Chaos
Shortbread and Sorrow
Espresso and Evil
Macarons and Mayhem

A Peridale Cafe MYSTERY

Book Six

CHAPTER 1

"Cheap, sugar-filled *nonsense*!" Dot exclaimed, turning to face the room as she crushed a Happy Bean coffee cup in her fist. "This is *not* what Peridale is about."

There was a murmur of agreement among the dozen people in the village hall. Barker squeezed Julia's hand reassuringly as they listened from the front seats.

"We *cannot* let these corporate bullies push us

Agatha Frost

around!" Dot cried, tossing the cup vehemently to the floor. "We *must* protect our way of life!"

Julia looked around the village hall, glad to see some of the familiar faces she hadn't seen since the new chain coffee shop had sprung up in the village, seemingly overnight.

"You may nod your head *now*, Amy Clark, but you're no better than the rest of them!" Dot pulled a small notepad from the breast pocket of her white blouse, licked her finger, and flicked through the pages until she landed on what she was looking for. "I saw you on Thursday, walking to the library with one of *their* cups in your hand!"

Amy Clark dropped her head and glanced apologetically at Julia. She smiled back to try and let her know it was okay, even if she did feel a little betrayed.

"And *you*, Shilpa Patil!" Dot cried, turning on her heels and extending a finger into the sea of faces as she flicked to the next page. "Don't think I didn't see you sneaking back into the post office with one of *their* sandwiches!"

Shilpa opened her mouth to defend herself before catching Julia's eyes and joining Amy in looking down at the floor.

"Processed *rubbish!*" Dot exclaimed as she

Espresso and Evil

tucked the notepad back into her blouse. She began to pace the small village hall as she adjusted the brooch holding her stiff collar in place, her pleated skirt fluttering side to side and her sensible shoes clicking on the polished wooden floor. "Doesn't this village mean *anything* to any of you?"

There was another murmur as all eyes landed on the floor. Julia wasn't sure if it was from remorse or out of fear of what Dot would do if they continued to stare at her.

"It's open a lot later than Julia's café," Father David offered, still in his black robes and dog collar. "I'm usually at the church late in the evenings."

"And it's cheaper," Imogen Carter dared to mumble. "Julia doesn't make chai lattes, and I really like them."

"You only had to ask," Julia said, the hurt evident in her voice. "I would make anything for any of you. You should know that."

They squirmed in their seats, glancing guiltily at each other. Harriet Barnes from the florist mouthed an apology to Julia, which she was grateful for. Julia clenched Barker's hand tightly, turning back to her gran as Dot stared out at the room with crossed arms and pursed lips.

"When that place opened up two weeks ago, you

Agatha Frost

all *swore* you wouldn't desert my granddaughter!" Dot started again, her tone suddenly softer. "But one by one, like sheep being led to slaughter, you've betrayed the only woman in this village who has been there for every single one of you since her café opened! Two years of service, and for what?"

"*Gran*," Julia said with a shake of her head. "That's enough."

"No, she's *right*, Julia!" Jessie, Julia's young apprentice and lodger cried, jumping up from her seat next to her. "You said it yourself! The café's sales have never been so low!"

Julia squirmed uncomfortably in her seat, her cheeks blushing from embarrassment. She had been ignoring that the sales had barely been covering the bills since the coffee shop had opened across the village green, but hearing Jessie say the words aloud only cemented how much trouble her business was in.

"It's not *just* us!" Emily Burns, Julia's closest neighbour called out. "The tourists have been going there too."

"But it's not the tourists who keep the café afloat when it's cold, or raining," Dot said, pinching between her eyes. "It's *you* people. The villagers. Julia's café is the beating heart of Peridale, and *you're*

Espresso and Evil

happy to watch it die."

"We came to this meeting, didn't we?" Amy Clark, the elderly organist from the church said, suddenly sitting up, her brows furrowed. "Why else would we be here if we didn't care?"

"Because *she* threatened to cut the heads off my beloved roses!" Emily said, pointing at Dot.

"And she told me she'd start catching the bus to a post office out of the village if I didn't come!" Shilpa said. "I'm a local business too!"

"Do you serve coffee, Shilpa?" Dot asked.

"Well, no, but –"

"Then this meeting isn't about you!" Dot snapped as she began to pace back and forth again. "Do you people want to help, or not?"

"What can we do?" Emily asked.

A devious grin spread across Dot's face. She scurried across the hall to the table at the side of the room, which usually contained refreshments for the different village meetings. Instead of refreshments, there were two large brown cardboard boxes that Julia hadn't noticed until now.

"We *protest*!" Dot announced as she pulled a Stanley knife from her small handbag. "This Saturday!"

Julia's heart sank to the pit of her stomach. She

exhaled and looked up at the ceiling, wondering if the last two weeks had been nothing more than a cruel nightmare. When she looked back at Dot as she sliced the knife down the tape holding the box together, she knew it was all too real. She had dreamed of owning a café since she was a little girl, and she could feel that dream decaying crumb by crumb.

"Isn't that illegal?" Amy asked, shifting in her seat. "I'm not going to prison for the sake of a café, no offence, Julia."

Julia shook her head to let her know no offence was taken.

"It's not illegal if we don't block the road, harass people, or stop entry to the building," Barker announced, letting go of Julia's hand to stand up and face the group. "I've already asked a couple of boys at the station to supervise, and they're more than happy to help."

Julia stared curiously at Barker, and then at Jessie. It was clear Dot had already let them in on her plans. Dot pulled a white t-shirt out of the box and let it hang proudly down her front.

"'*Choose Local Coffee*'," Dot announced, reading upside down from the black slogan on the t-shirt. "I got the idea from that campaign George Michael did

Espresso and Evil

in the eighties. We wear these on Saturday, and we let people know that there is an *alternative* to that soulless machine! Are you getting all of this, Johnny?"

Johnny Watson, who had been scribbling down everything Dot had just said for an article for *The Peridale Post* looked up and nodded. He adjusted his glasses and returned to his note taking.

"I *foresaw* this would happen!" Evelyn from the B&B announced as she clutched at the glittery brooch holding her purple turban in place, apparently channelling her psychic powers once more. "The cards mentioned a disruption in the village! I should have taken them more *seriously*!"

People looked awkwardly at each other as Evelyn began to hum and rock back and forth with her fingers pressed at her temples. As though to provide a distraction, Barker dragged off his tie and unbuttoned his shirt to reveal that he was already wearing one of the t-shirts. Jessie pulled off her black hoody and stood defiantly next to Barker in her own t-shirt.

"This is *important*," Jessie called out, planting her hands on her hips. "Whether you like it or not, you're all responsible for keeping local businesses open. Who is with us?"

Agatha Frost

A couple of people mumbled, but nobody immediately stood up. Julia looked out into the sea of faces, wondering if any of them would have come if Dot hadn't threatened them. Emily Burns eventually stood up, dragging Amy Clark up with her. Julia's heart warmed a little.

"Of course, we are with you, Julia," Emily called out, looking encouragingly at the others. "We just didn't realise the harm we were doing."

"I only really drink Moroccan tea, but I'm sure you'll put that on the menu if I give you some more," Evelyn said as she darted up, her purple caftan fluttering dramatically around her. "I'm with you! The cards predicted I would join a cause this week. How *exciting*!"

One by one the people in the room stood up and stepped forwards to collect a t-shirt from Dot. As they passed Julia, they all mumbled their apologies with their t-shirts clenched in their hands.

"Is this a private meeting or can anybody join?" a voice called from the back of the room, turning everyone's heads.

When Julia saw Anthony Kennedy's face, she suddenly felt sick. Jessie stepped forward, her fists clenched by her side, but Barker put out a hand to hold her back.

Espresso and Evil

"You are *not* welcome here," Dot called, pushing through the crowd so that she was face to face with the man who had brought Happy Bean to the village. "*Get out!*"

"'*Choose Local Coffee*'?" Anthony read aloud, a smirk tickling his lips as he ran his fingers through his blow-dried blonde hair. "You realise I am local, don't you? I was born in this village, and I've lived here for sixty-two years!"

Barker wrapped his hand around Julia's again, squeezing harder than ever before. She was unable to look at the man who was single-handily destroying her business.

"You're a *traitor!*" Dot cried, wagging a finger in his face. "This village isn't about franchises and corporations. It's about *real* people. You know how much Julia loves that café!"

"It's not personal," he said, stepping around Dot to look at Julia. "It's *just* business."

Julia avoided Anthony's eyes. She knew the betrayal hurt so bitterly because her gran was right; Anthony did know how much Julia had always wanted to run her own café.

"You were the best man at Julia's father's wedding!" Dot announced, turning back to the crowd to make sure they were listening. "You've

Agatha Frost

known her since the day she was born. This *is* personal."

Julia's stomach squirmed uncomfortably. She wanted nothing more than to retreat to the safety of her cottage and bury her head in some baking to take her away from the stress.

"Julia, love," Anthony called out, stepping around Dot. "It *is* just business!"

Daring to look up, Julia met Anthony's eyes, but she didn't see an ounce of compassion or remorse in his eyes, she just saw the cold and ruthless gaze she had come to know from the man. She looked away, scared she was going to say something she would regret in front of the people who were here to help her.

Anthony laughed coldly and dropped his gaze. He turned on the spot, his Cuban heels squeaking on the polished floor. Before he reached the door, he stopped in his tracks and looked into the crowd. He opened his mouth to speak, before shaking his head and marching out of the village hall as he pulled a packet of cigarettes from his jacket's inside pocket. Julia looked in the direction of what had caught Anthony's attention. She was surprised to see Anthony's teenage son, Gareth Kennedy, among the faces there to support her.

Espresso and Evil

"How do you even know that guy?" Jessie asked. "He's a slime ball."

"He was my father's business partner," Julia said as her heart rate slowed down. "They ran the antique barn together."

Julia swallowed a lump in her throat, knowing he had been much more than that. She had called him Uncle Anthony, even after she had figured out that he wasn't really her uncle. He was as much a part of her childhood memories as her mother and father, or Dot and her sister, Sue.

"Come to *spy*?" Dot asked Gareth, marching towards him in a similar fashion she had his father. "You can get out too!"

"I agree with you," Gareth said, catching Julia's eye. "It's not right what he's done."

Julia didn't know Gareth that well, but she appreciated the support all the same. He was seventeen, the same age as Jessie, and had come to Anthony and his wife, Rosemary, later in life, which had surprised everyone, including Julia. Anthony had never made it a secret that he never had any desire to have children.

Dot pursed her lips at the young boy before throwing him a t-shirt and scurrying back to the front of the group. Gareth looked down at the shirt in his hands as he chewed the inside of his cheek. There was no denying he was his father's son. Gareth's hair might have been styled a little more modern than his father's blow-dried mullet, but it was still the same golden hue. They also shared the same blue eyes, strong nose and jaw, and broad frame.

"We'll meet at midday on Saturday!" Dot announced, waving her hands to hush the chattering group. "*Spread the word*! We need all of the people we can get."

There was a final murmur of agreement before people filtered out of the room. When they were alone in the village hall, Julia let out a sigh of relief as she sat back in her seat.

"Are you sure this is a good idea?" she asked, looking down at the t-shirt in her hands. "It seems a little extreme."

"You've worked *too* hard for this," Dot said, sitting next to Julia and taking her hand. "This was all you talked about as a little girl. Even when you were in London for all those years, you'd still tell me on the phone how you were desperate to run your own café one day, even if Jerrad didn't care about what you wanted."

Dot suddenly bit her tongue, her eyes widening

Espresso and Evil

when she realised what she had said. They both turned to Barker, who looked confused at the pair of them.

"Who's Jerrad?" he asked quickly.

Julia opened her mouth, unsure of what to say. It had been five months since she had met Barker, but the time had never felt right to tell him about her twelve-year marriage. Her cheeks burned brightly as her mind turned to soup.

"*Did I miss it?*" Sue called out as she hurried into the village hall, her hands in the small of her back with her small bump poking out of her blue nurse's uniform. "The traffic was *murde*r!"

An audible sigh of relief left the mouths of Jessie, Dot, and Julia. Glad of the distraction, Julia hurried over and kissed Sue on the cheek before passing her a t-shirt.

"We're protesting," Julia said, glancing at Barker out of the corner of her eyes as he continued to stare suspiciously at her. "On Saturday. How's the shrimp?"

"According to Neil, it's now the size of a lime," Sue said as she rubbed the small, yet definite bump. "He's been reading books in the library, bless him, although it feels more like a melon at the moment. I have my twelve-week scan next week."

Agatha Frost

The conversation stayed firmly on Sue's pregnancy while they stacked the chairs. As they left the bright lights of the village hall and walked out into the warm summer's evening, it hadn't gone unnoticed by Julia that Barker was unusually silent.

"Don't worry, Julia," Dot said, squeezing Julia's shoulders as she looked across the village green at her dark café. "We'll fix this."

She smiled and nodded, turning her attention to the coffee shop, which was still illuminating the village green. Half a dozen people were lining up at the counter to get their drinks, some of them clutching white t-shirts in their hands.

Sue climbed into her car, and Dot hurried across the village green towards her cottage, leaving the three of them standing outside the village hall. Julia glanced at her aqua blue Ford Anglia, which was still parked next to her café. She pulled her keys from her pocket and turned to Barker, expecting him to repeat his question from earlier.

"Let's get a takeaway," Barker said, setting off towards Julia's car. "I'm starving."

"I want Indian," Jessie said, nudging Barker in the ribs with her elbow. "You picked last time. Can I drive home, Julia?"

"You failed your test!" Barker said with a

Espresso and Evil

chuckle as he climbed into the passenger seat of the car. "You almost killed that woman!"

"She was faking it," Jessie mumbled with a roll of her eyes as she sat in the back seat. "I *barely* hit her."

Julia pushed her key into the ignition. Her heart fluttered as she breathed freely, glad he had chosen not to push the subject at that moment. She knew she had to tell Barker the truth about her divorce eventually, but the longer she left it, the harder she knew it would be to reveal the only thing she had been keeping from him.

As she drove past Happy Bean, she dared to throw a glance in its direction. Her heart skipped a beat when she spotted Anthony staring out at them in the dark, his eyes trained on her car. A cold shudder ran down her spine. Even though she was hopeful, it felt like it was going to take more than a protest to turn her fortunes around.

CHAPTER 2

Julia rose with the sun on Saturday morning. She had nervously baked four different cakes and over fifty cupcakes before Jessie's alarm rang, which she subsequently ignored for almost ten minutes before finally dragging herself out of bed. She grunted at Julia as she stumbled into the bathroom, the hood of her black dressing gown pulled low over her scruffy hair and half-closed eyes.

Espresso and Evil

While Jessie showered, Julia made two cups of peppermint and liquorice tea. It had become a ritual for them to drink Julia's favourite tea with breakfast as they discussed the day ahead, even if Jessie never finished a full cup. Julia's hands were shaking with nerves, but she wanted to keep things as normal as possible for the both of them, even if the sky was falling in.

She sipped the tea, and its familiar sweetness soothed her. Mowgli, her grey Maine Coon, squeezed through the open kitchen window and padded across the counter towards her, leaving behind a trail of muddy paw prints and bringing in the scent of lavender from the garden. He nudged her, before jumping down to his bowl and loudly meowing. She grabbed a pouch of food from Mowgli's cupboard and squeezed half of the meat into his bowl. A knock at the door startled them both.

Julia looked up at the cat clock above her fridge with its swinging tail and darting eyes. It was only a little after seven. She scratched the top of Mowgli's head before walking down the hallway and to the front door.

Through the frosted glass, she saw a tall, broad man. The lack of a red jacket let her know it was probably a little early for the postman. She pulled her soft dressing gown across her pink silk pyjamas, tucked her curly hair behind her ears, and unlocked the door.

"*Dad?*" she said, the surprise loud in her voice. "What are doing here?"

Julia's father, Brian, smiled awkwardly down at her as he glanced back at his car, which he had parked behind her own. His expensive vehicle only served to highlight how dated her vintage wheels were.

"Your gran called," he said, reminding Julia that he rarely referred to her as '*mother*'. "She told me what was happening with Anthony."

"*Oh*," Julia mumbled, unsure of what to say. "Do you want to come in?"

He nodded, so she stepped to the side to let him into her cottage. He wiped his feet on the doormat as he looked around the house he had never visited before, despite Julia having been living back in Peridale for well over two years now.

"You've got a nice place," he said with a nervous laugh as he closed the door behind him. "Your mother would have loved this."

Julia's stomach squirmed at the mention of her mother, but she smiled all the same. Her

Espresso and Evil

relationship with her father had improved in recent months, but it didn't erase their years of being practically estranged after her mother's death all those years ago.

"How's Katie?" Julia asked as she led her father through to the kitchen, avoiding referring to her father's wife as her '*step-mother*'. "Tea?"

"Yes, please," he said as he took a seat in one of the stools at the counter, his head almost touching the low-beamed ceiling. "She's doing really well. Recovered from all of that business with her brother."

Julia refilled the kettle. It felt like a lifetime ago that Katie's brother, Charles, had been murdered during a garden party at their home. He had been protesting Katie's plans to turn their family manor into a spa, and it had been Julia who had uncovered the culprit after falsely accusing Katie of her brother's murder. Months had passed, and spring had turned to summer, but Julia hadn't seen her father, or Katie since, which made his appearance at her cottage feel stranger.

"I was surprised to hear from your gran," he said as she handed him a cup of tea. "Did you put sugar in this?"

"You've always taken two sugars."

"Katie's got me on no-sugar," he said with an apologetic shrug. "Thinks I'm at risk of diabetes because of my age."

Julia took back the cup and tossed it down the drain, not needing another reminder that her father was sixty-four, and his wife was thirty-seven, just like Julia. She quickly remade the tea before leaning against the sink with her own tea.

"You know I don't get into the village much, so I was surprised to hear what Anthony had done," he said after taking a sip of the hot tea. "The rumour mill doesn't seem to make its way up to Peridale Manor. I wanted to show my support and let you know that I'm here for you."

Jessie appeared in the bathroom doorway, a towel tucked under her armpits with her wet hair hanging over her face. Brian turned in his seat, causing Jessie to scurry off to her bedroom.

"Still got the lodger?" he asked as he turned back.

"She's more than that," Julia said, her tone sharper than she intended. "Jessie is like family to me."

Brian nodded and took another sip of his tea. Julia could have cut the tension between them with a knife. Despite the man in front of her being her

Espresso and Evil

father, they were practically strangers to each other. After her mother's death, he had buried himself in his work, travelling the country hunting for antiques while Anthony ran the shop. Julia had learned very young not to rely on the man.

"Why are you surprised Anthony would do something like this?" Julia asked, looking down at Mowgli as he chewed his food contently, unbothered by the presence of the stranger in his house. "We both know he's always been a ruthless businessman."

"And not a very good one," he said, leaning forward and clasping his fingers together. "The man conned me out of my share of the business we built together, but last I heard he was almost broke."

"He must have come into some money," Julia said, not wanting to admit she had researched the staggering amount it would cost to start a Happy Bean franchise. "You know it only takes a couple of decent antiques to turn things around."

"That's just the thing. The man was completely useless," he admitted, cupping his hands around the mug as he stared down into the golden surface of the tea. "Wouldn't know a Shigaraki Kiln Soy Vase from a Zsolnay. It was always my knowledge that propped the business up. I told him how much things were worth, and he sold them with his charm and charisma. He was good at that. Always had the gift of the gab, that's for sure."

"Well, he's certainly doing his best to make sure he's eliminating the competition," Julia whispered after sipping her tea.

Brian pulled his wallet out of his pocket and looked down at it for a second, weighing it up in his hands. He pulled it open to reveal that it was bursting with more red fifty-pound notes than Julia had ever seen in one place. He pulled them all out and pushed them across the counter.

"Your gran said you were struggling," he said, tapping a finger on the cash. "It's not a lot, but it'll tide you over."

Julia couldn't decide if she was offended or flattered. She stared down at the money, her mouth ajar. It would help, but she couldn't help but think the money had come from Katie's family fortune and not his pocket. After all, he had admitted that Anthony had conned him out of his business and Julia knew he hadn't worked since marrying Katie over five years ago. It wasn't like he needed to. Katie was sitting on the Wellington fortune, and with her brother dead and her father wheelchair bound, it wasn't going to be long before she inherited the family pot of gold.

Espresso and Evil

Before she could respond, Jessie came out of her bedroom dressed for work, already wearing her protest t-shirt. She hovered back before Julia gave her a supportive nod. She walked cautiously forward and sat at the counter, leaving a seat between them. She reached out for her tea, her eyes widening when she spotted the money.

"I should get going," he said, standing up and pushing his unfinished tea away as he checked his gold watch, no doubt designer. "Katie will be wondering where I've gone. She told me to invite you and your sister to lunch next Sunday."

"I'll let Sue know," she said, not giving him a definite answer as she wondered if it was really Katie who had asked that. "I'll show you out."

She walked her father to the door, leaving Jessie with her tea in the kitchen. When they reached the door, he turned and opened his mouth, but closed it again.

"I appreciate you coming to see me," Julia whispered, resting a hand on his shoulder. "You're always welcome here, you know that."

"I know," he said, his fingers closing around the door handle as though he couldn't wait to get back to his manor. "Just be careful today. Anthony won't think twice about playing dirty."

Her father left her cottage and walked back to his car. Before he drove away, he waved, and she waved back. When he drove down the winding lane, she exhaled, hating how awkward things were with the man she had adored as a child. She looked out to Emily Burns' cottage across the road. She waved with her rose pruning shears in her hands. Just like Jessie, she too was already in her '*Choose Local Coffee*' t-shirt. Julia waved back a little less enthusiastically as Emily craned her neck to see if she recognised the car speeding away from them.

"There's five hundred quid here," Jessie said, wafting the red notes in her hand. "He must be minted."

Julia sighed and took the money from Jessie. She hadn't wanted to keep it, but she hadn't been able to bring herself to flat out refuse either.

"I forgot to give it back," Julia said, unsure if that was true. She flicked through the notes before rolling them up and stuffing the bundle in the biscuit tin with the custard creams. "Hopefully, we won't need it."

***

"*SAVE PERIDALE!*" DOT'S VOICE CRACKLED out of the megaphone and floated through the open

Espresso and Evil

café door. "This faceless coffee shop is *destroying* local businesses!"

If Julia wasn't completely rushed off her feet trying to keep up with her full café's orders, she might have asked her gran to calm down a little. Even though things had started off quietly and it had just been Dot and a couple of her friends outside the coffee shop, there were now over twenty people there, all wearing the t-shirts, and holding signs written out in Dot's handwriting.

"If you want *real* coffee, go to my granddaughter's café," Dot cried out. "*Real* coffee, made by *real* people. Support local business!"

"We've not been this busy in weeks!" Jessie whispered excitedly as she hurried past Julia with a tray of tea and scones for a group of women who were curiously staring around Julia's café. "Dot's nutty plan *actually* worked!"

Julia took down another large food order and hurried through to the kitchen, where Sue was spreading butter on bread rolls as fast as she could.

"Not how I thought I'd be spending my first Saturday off in months," Sue said as she dabbed at her red face with a tea towel. "I bet they can hear her in Timbuktu!"

Julia hurried back through to the café, pleased to

see Barker pushing through the crowd and making his way towards her.

"It's nice to see this place full again," he said as he approached the counter, his eyes darting up to the chalkboard menu behind her. "I'll take a large Americano to go. I'm on the clock."

"It's just one day, but it's a good sign."

"Your gran is certainly determined," Barker said with a chuckle as he pulled change from his pocket. "She needs to watch what she's saying though. She's crossing the line between protest and slander, and if Anthony officially complains, she could be arrested."

Julia pitied the poor officer who would try to put cuffs on Dot. Her gran might have been eighty-three, but she was the feistiest and most exuberant woman in the village. Her tongue may have been razor sharp, but the fact she had organised this protest to try and help Julia only proved how big her heart was.

She quickly made Barker's Americano and bagged up a chocolate cupcake for him to take away. When he reached into his pocket to grab more change, she rested her hand on his to stop him.

"You more than deserve it," Julia said, pushing the bag into his hand. "It's the least I can do."

"I didn't do anything," Barker said as he peeled

Espresso and Evil

off the plastic lid from his coffee to add a sachet of brown sugar. "When Dot told me her plan, there was no way I wasn't going to help. I know how much you love this place, and I love you, so it was a no-brainer."

He leaned across the counter to give her a quick kiss before pulling away with a playful smirk, his teeth biting his lips. He turned on his heels and headed for the door with his coffee and cupcake, making way for more customers to walk into Julia's café.

"Take these outside," Julia said, handing Jessie a tray with an assortment of cupcakes on them. "Free samples. People might be in here today, but we want them to come back."

Jessie finished making a latte before taking the tray, hurrying through the café and out onto the village green. As Julia watched her approach the people to offer them free cupcakes with a smile, pride swelled through her. It hadn't been that long ago that Jessie had been homeless and breaking into Julia's café for her cakes. Julia didn't want to take any credit for Jessie's transformation, but she was glad she had given her a chance that she might not have gotten otherwise.

"Who's that boy talking to Jessie?" Sue asked as

she appeared behind her with a plate of sandwiches for one of the tables. "He's a little close."

Julia squinted into the sun at the boy. Even though she couldn't see his face, the red tracksuit and baseball cap gave him away.

"Billy Matthews," Julia answered. "He's quite smitten with Jessie. I don't think she wants to admit that she likes him too. He's persistent."

"Is that the serial killer's kid?" Sue asked on her way back, pausing to grab one of the cupcakes from the cake stand. "The one that Barker sent to prison all those years ago before he moved to Peridale and left that funeral wreath on Barker's doorstep as a threat before a man was actually murdered? I'm surprised you're letting her associate herself with people like that."

"Jeffrey Taylor was found innocent," Julia reminded her. "He's an okay guy. Barker and he have gone for a few pints in The Plough since. I think it's more to prove that there's no bad blood between them. Jeffrey is trying to set a good example for Billy."

"Didn't Billy put a brick through your café's window?" Sue mumbled through a mouthful of cake as she arched a brow. "And didn't he try to steal your handbag too?"

Espresso and Evil

Julia watched as Jessie walked away from Billy, but he followed her like a lovesick puppy. Jessie tossed her hair over her shoulder and shouted something at him, which only made him laugh and follow her even closer.

"He's not been in trouble with the police for months," Julia said tactfully. "You shouldn't judge a book by its cover. Everybody deserves a second chance."

"Speaking of books, Neil got this book from the library that said my lime is going to turn into a small pumpkin," Sue said uneasily as she rested a hand on her small stomach. "A *pumpkin*, Julia! I don't think I thought this through."

"You're going to be fine," Julia reassured her. "If it were that bad, Mum would have stopped with me."

Sue looked like she was about to argue, but she appeared to think about it for a second before mentally agreeing with Julia. She hurried back into the kitchen to start on the next order, leaving Julia to continue to watch Jessie and Billy. Her heart stopped when she spotted Anthony marching out of his coffee shop and across the village green towards Jessie, his open shirt flapping against his bronzed chest in the summer breeze. He tiptoed awkwardly on top of the grass as though he didn't want to get his expensive shoes dirty. Without a second thought, Julia abandoned her post and joined him in running towards Jessie.

"You need a permit to hand out street food," Anthony exclaimed smugly as he shielded his eyes from the sun with one hand while the other clicked at Jessie like she was a dog about to perform a trick. "I *assume* you have the right paperwork from the council?"

"Kiss my –"

"*Jessie!*" Julia cried, interrupting her before she said something Anthony could use against her. "Go back to the café. I'll deal with this."

"I could take him," Billy offered as he cracked his knuckles. "I've knocked out bigger."

"*Billy!*" Julia cried. "You get to the café too. What would your dad say?"

Billy scowled at Julia before rolling his eyes at the same time as Jessie. Despite Jessie's protests that she couldn't stand Billy, they were more alike than Jessie would like to admit.

"Aren't you going to offer me one?" Anthony asked, reaching out for the tray.

Jessie swiftly pulled it out of his way, but not before he managed to grab one of the red velvet

Espresso and Evil

cupcakes. He took a step back and began to slowly unpeel the casing, making sure to take his time to peel the paper away from each ridge in the tiny cake. Dot and the rest of the protestors had suddenly gone silent and were making their way across the village green towards them.

"Looks *delicious*," he mocked, winking at Julia. "Did you bake this yourself, Julia?"

"Julia bakes *everything* herself," Dot announced through the megaphone. "*Everything* at Julia's café is home baked! Unlike Happy Bean's cakes, which are *filled* with chemicals and have shelf-lives that will outlive the cockroaches and Cher herself!"

The people who had been making their way across to Julia's café stopped to observe the commotion. Julia watched as Anthony slowly lifted the cake up to his lip, his eye contact unwavering. It unsettled her that this was a man she had known since the day she was born, and yet she saw none of that recognition in his icy blue eyes.

"Get on with it, man!" Billy cried, stepping forward and cracking his knuckles again. "You're not getting any younger."

Anthony bit into the cake, and Julia was surprised to see the same look of pleasure she would expect to see from one of her paying customers. For a moment, she thought her baking had worked at healing the rift between her café and the new coffee shop, and she almost felt foolish for not trying to work with the new business, rather than against it.

But suddenly, Anthony's face contorted, as though he had just bit into a sour wedge of lemon. He crushed the cake between his teeth painfully slowly as a hand reached up to his mouth. A gasp rattled through the crowd when he pulled something red and shiny from between his lips. He wiped the wet cake mixture off it and held it up to the sun.

"*A red fingernail!*" Anthony explained, barely able to hide the smugness in his voice as he twisted the piece of acrylic in the light. "As you heard yourself, ladies and gentlemen, Julia *does* bake everything herself. We might buy our cakes from the wholesaler at Happy Bean, but I can *assure* you, we follow the most *basic* food safety standards."

Julia looked at Jessie, who looked as confused as she felt. Julia lifted up her fingers, but they were natural and free of any nail polish, as were Jessie's.

"I don't even wear fake nails!" Julia cried. "He *planted* that!"

"You *all* saw me!" Anthony said, directing his attention to the gathering crowd. "I couldn't have possibly planted anything in that cake."

Espresso and Evil

"You're gonna pay for –" Billy cried, launching himself forward, only to be to dragged back by Jessie.

"I'll leave you to make up your minds," Anthony said with a sneer, tossing his hands out as he turned back to his coffee shop. "I gather you're all *intelligent* people."

Anthony pocketed the nail and screwed up the cupcake wrapper before dropping it to the grass. Julia watched in disbelief as he sauntered slowly back to his coffee shop, followed by most of the people who had been standing and watching. They were all looking at Julia in disgust, but she couldn't summon the words to defend herself. Her father had been right about Anthony being a good salesman and a dirty player.

"Emily! Amy! *Plan B*!" Dot cried through the megaphone before she tossed it to the ground and set off running towards the coffee shop, overtaking Anthony and the customers in a flash.

Before anybody could figure out what was going on, Emily and Amy stepped forward, pulling long metal chains from their tiny handbags. Dot stood in front of the coffee shop and in an instant, as though it had been rehearsed, Emily and Amy chained Dot's arms and legs to the front of the coffee shop before padlocking them in place.

"*Wicked*," Jessie whispered with a grin.

"That woman has *style*," Billy said, as he draped an arm around Jessie's shoulders. "I can still punch him for you, if you want, babe?"

"Shut up," Jessie said as she rolled her eyes and tossed his arm away. "Here comes trouble."

Jessie nodded in the direction of two uniformed officers who had been watching the protest unfold. They walked over to Emily and Amy, presumably asking for the keys to the padlocks, but they both shrugged, before linking arms and hurrying up the lane towards Emily's cottage.

"I will *not* be moved!" Dot cried. "This is a *peaceful* protest!"

"What about when she needs to pee?" Jessie whispered into Julia's ears as they walked across the village green. "Won't her arms get tired?"

Julia didn't know what to say. She turned back to her café, which was emptying as though the building was on fire. Sue darted between the tables trying to make them stay, but it was no use. She exhaled heavily, wondering how things could have gone so dramatically wrong.

It only took a couple of minutes for one of the officers to arrive with a pair of bolt cutters to cut

Espresso and Evil

Dot down. The trapped customers inside of the coffee shop scurried out, only to be replaced with the ones trying to flee Julia's café after seeing her contaminated cakes.

"*Call my lawyer!*" Dot cried as they pulled her arms behind her back and handcuffed them in place. "*Call the press!*"

Julia pinched uncomfortably between her brows as the officers forced Dot into the back of a police car. Barker mouthed his apology to her, with a look of '*I told you so*', but she shook her head to let him know it wasn't his fault.

The second Dot was driven towards the police station, the protest party dispersed, smiling their awkward apologies to Julia. She wasn't angry with them for leaving; she would have done the same. They had tried, and that mattered to her.

"Are they going to charge her?" Jessie asked.

"I doubt it," Julia said. "I'm sure Barker will do his best, although he might want to make her sweat a little first."

Julia turned her attention to Anthony, who was sitting at one of the sterile metallic tables outside his coffee shop, smoking a cigarette as he watched the scene come to an end. He looked mildly amused more than anything. It hurt Julia that somebody could be so callous and care so little.

Julia spotted Anthony's wife, Rosemary Kennedy, storm out of the coffee shop towards her husband, wearing one of Happy Bean's barista uniforms with her greying hair pinned at the back of her head in a tight roll. Julia was sure the woman was past retirement age. He grabbed her wrist and pulled her in, attempting to kiss her on the cheek, but she tugged her arm away and stormed off. She yanked her apron over her head and tossed it to the ground before tossing her hands in the air. Julia noticed her red nails, particularly the lack of one on her left index finger. Anthony chuckled and shook his head as though that too amused him.

"What now?" Jessie whispered as the crowd disappeared, leaving them alone on the village green.

Julia looked back at her café, her heart heavy. She thought about the five hundred pounds in her biscuit tin at her cottage, the likelihood that she would need to use her father's money increasing. Julia linked arms with Jessie, and they set off back towards her café.

Before she reached the door, she turned back and looked at Happy Bean. A man had joined Anthony at the table with two coffees in their signature white and green cups. Anthony offered the

Espresso and Evil

man a cigarette, but he declined with a wave of his hand and a toothy smile. Julia's heart stopped for a moment. Did she recognise that smile? She shielded her eyes and squinted across the village, but her heart eased when she realised it was her imagination playing tricks on her.

"Too much hair," she whispered to herself as she shook away the suggestion.

"*Huh?*" Jessie asked.

"Nothing," Julia said, wrapping her arm around Jessie's shoulder as they walked back into the café. "Let's clean up. You never know, there might be a second wind."

Jessie nodded enthusiastically, even if both of them knew it was more than a little unlikely. As she gathered the half-finished sandwiches and cakes from the tables, she looked around her café, wondering if her dream was coming to an end. If her gran's protest couldn't save her café against the corporate machine, she didn't know what would. She wasn't going to hold her breath for a miracle.

CHAPTER 3

Later that night Julia was on her sitting room floor with Jessie, and her two new college friends, Dolly and Dom.

"I promise it won't hurt," Dom said as he smeared the jet-black charcoal face mask on Jessie's face. "Just sit *still*."

Julia attempted to chuckle as Jessie squirmed under Dom's forceful touch, but he had already

Espresso and Evil

attacked Julia with the black mask ten minutes ago, and it had completely frozen her face.

"Is it meant to burn?" Jessie asked when Dom had finished.

"Drama queen," Dolly said as she rolled onto her back on the hearthrug, the spoon from the ice cream tub still in her mouth. "We saw Billy earlier."

Jessie's eyes darted to Julia, and then to her fingers, which were suddenly fiddling with the drawstrings on her black pyjama bottoms.

"*So?*" she replied, attempting and failing to frown through the face mask. "I don't care."

"You *so* love him," Dom said, ribbing her with his elbow. "I bet you're blushing under there."

He went to peel the mask, but Jessie batted his hand away and snatched the ice cream spoon from Dolly to fill her mouth with the chocolatey goodness. The sleepover had been Jessie's idea, but the ice cream had been Julia's. After the day she had endured, she needed the distraction and the dairy.

"It's almost midnight," Dom announced as he climbed onto the sofa and tossed his head upside down to squint at the clock on the mantelpiece. "Remember how Cinderella turned back into a witch at midnight? You're going to be the opposite when we're finished with you, Jessie!"

"She wasn't a witch," Dolly mumbled as she tapped her fingers against her black, frozen cheeks. "She was a slave."

"She was a servant," Jessie corrected them, much to everyone's surprise. "*What?* I grew up in foster care, not on the moon!"

Jessie's expression remained stern for a moment before she broke out laughing. They all attempted to chuckle, wincing through the pain of the masks that Dom had insisted would make them all look and feel ten years younger. Considering Julia had twenty years on the three of them, she wasn't sure how much younger they could look without having to crawl back into nappies.

"How's college?" Julia asked, fondly remembering her days in the patisserie and baking course. "Is Mr Jackson still there?"

"*Jacko?*" Dom asked. "He's properly ancient! He creaks when he walks."

"Leaves a trail of dust," Dolly cackled, amused by herself. "He's practically mummified."

Jessie joined in the laughing, which in turn made Julia laugh. When Jessie had first told her she had made friends at college, Julia had been a little surprised, not because she didn't think Jessie was capable of making friends, but because she didn't

Espresso and Evil

think Jessie would want to, especially with kids her own age. When Jessie brought Dolly and Dom to the cottage a couple of weeks ago, Julia had been even more surprised to see that her new friends were impossibly tall, platinum blonde twins who wore every colour in the rainbow at all times. Julia loved them. They always had something funny to say, and their spirits were so pure. She wasn't sure they could manage to say a bad word about anyone if they tried.

"If you're not going to chase after Billy, I might try," Dom said as he twirled a blonde curl around his index finger. "In for a penny."

"I'm not chasing anybody," Jessie mumbled with a roll of her eyes.

"*He's* chasing you though," Dolly exclaimed as she took the spoon from Jessie to dig out a huge brownie chunk. "What do you think of him, Julia?"

"Erm, he's – *nice*," Julia said, everything she knew about Billy racing through her mind. "He's growing up."

Jessie snorted her disagreement before snatching the spoon back from Dolly and finishing the last of the ice cream. Dom let out a long yawn, which was echoed by Dolly, and then Julia. Jessie seemed to be the only one who wasn't tired.

"Do you have any Saturday jobs at your café?"

Agatha Frost

Dom asked, looking at Julia upside down as he dangled off the edge of the sofa. "Our tutor at college said we should try and find Saturday jobs because the bakery we work at doesn't open on the weekends."

"No, there isn't," Jessie jumped in, her eyes darting uneasily at Julia. "I *told* you not to ask."

"In for a penny," Dom said again with a shrug and a smile, not fazed by the rejection. "I wonder what Billy is doing right now."

Jessie sighed and tossed the spoon into the ice cream tub. Julia thought Jessie was about to launch into an argument with Dom, but they were interrupted when Julia's mobile phone vibrated on the side table. They all jumped and looked at the phone, Dom and Dolly immediately bursting out laughing.

"It's *midnight*!" Dolly exclaimed. "Maybe that's Billy looking for his princess?"

Jessie picked up a cushion and launched it at Dolly, who didn't even try to dodge it. It hit her square in the face, which only caused more hysterical laughter, which was only interrupted by another yawn.

Julia rolled across the floor and grabbed her phone from the table. She looked down at the

Espresso and Evil

unknown contact and frowned, the mask pinching her forehead. It didn't resemble a phone number she had ever seen. She was about to reject the call and toss it back onto the table because of the late hour, but she suddenly remembered what the number was.

"It's the security alarm at the café," Julia mumbled under her breath. "It calls me when the alarm is triggered. Gran convinced me to get it after Billy put a brick through my window."

"Was it a *love* brick?" Dom asked, twiddling Jessie's hair.

"No, it was a *brick* brick," Jessie said, batting his hand away. "Is it serious, Julia?"

Julia answered the call, and as expected it gave her an automated message that her alarm had been triggered a minute before midnight. She glanced at the clock and sighed as she forced herself up off the rug, her knees creaking a little.

"Just stay here," Julia said as she headed for the door. "I won't be long. It's probably nothing."

Julia slipped her feet into her sheepskin slippers, tied her dressing gown around her waist, and grabbed her car keys.

"You've still got your mask on," Jessie mumbled through her tight face. "I'm coming with you."

"You're not," Julia said as she turned to the

Agatha Frost

hallway mirror to tug at the mask's edge. "*Ouch!* What is this made of?"

Jessie joined her in the mirror and tugged at her mask. She yelped, and immediately let go, tears lining her eyes.

"Satan's flesh," Jessie mumbled darkly. "Let's just rip it off. Like a plaster."

Julia nodded and met Jessie's eyes in the mirror. They both yanked up from the bottom of their cheeks, but they stopped before they had even passed their mouths. Julia wiped away the tears as they streamed down her glossy black cheeks.

"I'll wash it off when I get back," Julia said, blinking through the pain as her fingers closed around her car key. "You're not coming with me."

"They'll already be asleep," Jessie whispered. "*Please.*"

"It's been less than a minute," Julia said, walking past Jessie and back into the sitting room, where Dolly was fast asleep on the rug, and Dom was draped across the sofa with his hand on his stomach and his head still hanging over the edge, his mouth gaping open. "*Unbelievable.*"

"It's some freaky talent they have," Jessie said as she pulled her usual black hoody over her pyjamas. "It's probably a lack of things going on in their

Espresso and Evil

head."

Julia and Jessie shared a little grin for a second before she reluctantly opened the front door, letting Jessie walk through first. She locked Dolly and Dom in and walked towards her car, hoping they were heading towards nothing more than a false alarm.

"In for a penny," Julia whispered.

***

WHEN JULIA DROVE INTO THE VILLAGE, she immediately heard the blaring siren and saw the red flashing lights coming from her café. As she pulled up outside, the lights in the bedrooms across the village green flicked on, including her gran's, who had been released from the police station with a caution after only an hour of questioning.

"The door is open," Jessie mumbled as she scrambled for her seatbelt. "I'm going to *murder* whoever it is!"

Julia killed the engine and struggled to undo her seatbelt. She caught a glimpse of her shiny face in the rear-view mirror, realising how ridiculous she looked.

She slammed her car door and hurried over to her café. The small pane of glass in the door had been smashed, the fragments on the doormat. Pulling Jessie back, Julia edged into the dark café, immediately making her way to the alarm system. She punched in the code, which was the date she had rescued Mowgli, and the alarm finally stopped.

"*Hello?*" she called out into her empty café.

"Come out, you *rats*!" Jessie cried, bursting past Julia and running into the kitchen. "They've gone."

Julia hurried after her. To her relief, the kitchen was empty. She flicked on the light to see what had been taken but was surprised to see everything where she had left it, including all of her expensive professional baking equipment that had cost her a pretty penny when first opening. She turned and looked through the beads into the café, but the till was still there too.

"*Odd,*" Julia whispered. "Maybe it was an accident?"

"There's no such thing," Jessie said, storming out of the café and turning on her mobile phone's flashlight.

She scanned it across the village green, and down the alleyway between the café and the post office. Julia followed her, but she couldn't see anybody.

"Maybe a bird flew into the window?" Julia

Espresso and Evil

suggested.

"There's no blood," Jessie said bluntly. "Somebody is trying to scare you."

Before Julia could ask who, she looked over to Happy Bean, her stomach turning when she saw that all the lights were still on. She knew they opened late, but not this late.

"Get in the car," Julia ordered.

"*Fat chance!*"

"Jessie!"

"*What?*"

"Do as you're told."

"Have we met?" Jessie replied with a clenched jaw. "I'm not leaving your side, cake lady."

In their pyjamas and charcoal face masks, they edged towards their rival, sticking to each other's side like Velcro. Jessie illuminated the path in front of them, her Doc Martens clunking on the cobbled road underfoot. When they were feet from the coffee shop, Julia noticed that the door was slightly ajar.

"We should call the police," Julia whispered, holding her arm in front of Jessie. "This doesn't feel right."

Jessie pouted before stepping around Julia's arm. She set off straight for the door. To Julia's surprise, she pulled her sleeve over her hand before pushing on the door. Julia suddenly remembered the time she had caught Jessie breaking into her café before they had known each other, and she realised she had more expertise than Julia had given her credit for.

All the lights in the coffee shop were switched on, but it appeared empty. Julia followed Jessie inside for the first time, making sure not to touch anything. She looked around at what her competition had to offer, initially impressed until she took a couple of steps inside. Everything looked like it was trying impossibly hard to appear comfortable and relatable, but it all felt a little sterile. On closer inspection, the exposed brick walls were just wallpaper, the leather sofas were pleather, and the framed pictures on the walls were nothing more than generic stock photography and bland prints of utilitarian paintings. Even the menu above the counter was eerily barren, with calorie contents and prices in tiny black text, making her chalkboard menu look like a piece of art.

"Julia," Jessie said with a gulp as she peered over the counter. "You might want to see this."

Julia's heart suddenly stopped in her chest. She recognised the fear and shock in Jessie's eyes. She had felt it herself more times than she cared to remember recently.

Espresso and Evil

Taking her steps carefully and slowly, Julia walked towards the counter where Jessie was pointing the light. She looked over, and jumped back with a gasp, having not expected to see the eyes of Anthony Kennedy staring back up at her, glassy and vacant.

"Is he dead?" Jessie asked.

"I think so," Julia gulped, nodding her head as she dared to take another look. "We should get out of –"

Her voice trailed off when something on the counter caught her eye. She leaned in and peered at what had caught her attention, realising that it had been her own name. Perfectly aligned under the spotlight above the counter sat two sugar sachets, one brown and one white, both inscribed with glossy red writing.

"'*Murder*'," Julia read aloud, her throat drying up. "'*Julia did it*'. We really should get out of here."

To Julia's surprise, Jessie pressed a couple of buttons on her phone before taking a picture of the sugars. When Julia shook her head to ask her what she was doing, Jessie shrugged and pocketed her phone.

"It's *evidence*!" Jessie cried defensively. "It looks like it's been written in blood."

Agatha Frost

Julia took a step back, but something sharp pierced through her sheepskin slippers and stabbed into the sole of her foot. She yelped and jumped back. She looked down at a long metal screw, which was sticking up on the ground and covered in white dust. She felt her foot, but it didn't appear to be bleeding. Jessie bent down to pick up the screw, but Julia quickly held her back.

"Call the –"

Before Julia could finish her sentence, a hot light flooded the coffee shop. It took Julia a moment to realise that the burning brightness was coming from outside. They both turned around, their hands shielding their eyes from the white light. Julia opened her mouth to say something, but she couldn't see a thing beyond the brightness.

"*Come out with your hands up!*" a stern and angry voice cried over a megaphone. "*Don't try anything stupid!*"

As Julia walked towards the coffee shop door, she caught the reflection of their covered faces in the window. She knew things couldn't look any worse if they tried.

"There's a dead man in here," Julia called out, her hands above her head. "Somebody broke into my café across the village green, and I saw this door

Espresso and Evil

open and came to see what was happening. We haven't done anything wrong."

An officer stepped away from a police car, his baton in one hand and a pair of handcuffs in the other. Jessie shifted in closer to Julia, her hands also high above her head. Despite her bravado, Julia could feel fear radiating from every fibre of Jessie's being.

"We haven't done anything wrong," Julia repeated, daring to take a step forward as another officer circled the car, the headlights still blinding her.

"*Stay where you are!*" one of them called.

Before Julia knew what to do or say, both of them were in handcuffs and being driven past her café and through the village to the local police station, still in their increasingly tight charcoal face masks and pyjamas.

"We're done for, aren't we?" Jessie whispered.

"I think so," Julia replied, not knowing how she could sugar-coat their situation. "*I think so.*"

CHAPTER 4

The sun burned Julia's eyes as she stumbled out of the station with Jessie by her side. The moment she saw Barker sat on the bench outside the closed pub across the road, Julia ran straight into his arms, the tears lining her lashes.

"*Oh, Julia,*" he said as he clenched her face to his chest. "I came as soon as I heard."

"It was horrible," Julia whispered, her fingers

Espresso and Evil

clinging to the back of Barker's shirt. "They've been questioning us for most of the night."

"They wouldn't let me anywhere near the interview rooms. It's procedure when we're so close to a —"

"*Suspect*?" Jessie asked as she joined them outside The Plough. "You can say it."

Barker smiled sympathetically at Jessie before pulling away from Julia and holding her by the shoulders. He stared deep into her eyes, as though to calm her, but she could see the deep-set panic in his pupils.

"Why didn't you call me when the alarm went off?" Barker asked with a sigh. "I could have sorted this sooner."

"Sorted it?" Jessie asked.

"The only reason they've let you go without charging you is because I've been running around the village trying to prove your story. One of the girls at the station called me first thing this morning and told me everything that had happened, and how they were treating you like murder suspects. She said you were wearing balaclavas?"

"They were charcoal face masks," Julia said, her fingers drifting up to her still stinging cheeks after having the masks forcibly removed by the arresting officers. "*Dolly and Dom!*"

She clasped her fingers around her mouth as guilt surged through her. In all of the commotion, she had completely forgotten about the houseguests she had locked in her cottage.

"If you're talking about those two blonde kids asleep on your floor, they're still there," Barker said, a little confused. "They're curled up in a giant ball with Mowgli in the middle of them."

Julia pulled the plastic bag out of her pocket that contained her phone, car keys, and watch, the possessions that had been confiscated during her arrest. She squinted at the small watch face, surprised that it was already two in the afternoon. She looked around the village, suddenly realising that it was buzzing around her, and she was still in her pyjamas.

"I suppose they're just like two cats," Jessie said absently, her eyes glazing over as she stared into space. "Cats in clothes."

"How did you prove our story?" Julia asked as she reattached her watch. "They were acting like we had conspired to kill Anthony. They knew all about what happened with the fingernail earlier in the day, but that's Peridale for you."

"After that nasty business with the wreath on my

Espresso and Evil

doorstep, I had security cameras installed all around my cottage," Barker said nervously. "They caught you driving by at four minutes past midnight. I was banging on Shilpa's door at six this morning to get her post office footage. I don't think she likes me much right now, but it proves the rest of the story. You arrived in the village, went into your café, walked out and then went to Happy Bean. That's when the officers turned up. One of the residents called them when they heard your alarm. I have a good mind to have those jokers fired! They were one step away from tasering you, I'm sure of it!"

A cold shudder spread across Julia's shoulders. She pulled her dressing gown across her body and tucked her scruffy hair behind her ears, never one to be self-conscious, but also not one to wander around the village in her nightclothes.

"We're out now," Julia said, trying to force a smile. "That's all that matters."

"I'm not finished," Barker said, appearing a little excited and nervous at the same time. "The footage spotted somebody leaving Happy Bean, run to your café, and then head off into the night."

"Who?" Julia asked.

"I don't know," he said through a gritted jaw. "They were hooded. It's not the best quality. They went through the back door of the coffee shop, killed Anthony, and fled through the front. I've already checked, and there are no cameras covering the back entrance. If this were London, we'd have every corner covered, but it seems Peridale is quite resistant to surveillance."

Julia's mind flashed back to an uproar that had happened soon after she had moved back to the village. The council had been trying to erect cameras around the village green to target petty crime, but the backlash from the villagers had been so great, they had eventually backed down. It turned out the residents didn't like the thought of being spied on, which Dot had said was because everybody had something to hide.

"I just want to go home, shower, and sleep," Julia said after a long yawn, glad that it was Sunday, meaning she didn't have to think about her café. "I think we've earned it."

"There's more," Barker said, the concern growing in his voice. "They found something in the cake display case in your café."

"Found what?" Jessie asked loudly. "Because if it's a library book on American desserts, I swear I didn't know it was overdue!"

"They found a bottle of something," Barker said,

Espresso and Evil

his eyes meeting Julia's. "They've blocked me from this case, but I know the detective they've brought in from Cheltenham to lead the investigation, and he told me that their early tests suggest it's a poison of some kind."

"The murder weapon?" Jessie asked. "In Julia's café?"

"That explains the break-in," Julia theorised. "Why *my* café?"

Barker arched a brow and tucked his hands into his jacket. He cocked his head back and smirked dryly at her.

"You're taking this rather calmly," Barker said. "If I didn't know you, I'd think it was because you were involved, but I do know you, so what are you thinking?"

"Somebody is trying to frame me," Julia said, forcing down the lump in her throat. "I've had all night to come to that conclusion. The sugar at the scene proved that."

"Sugar?" Barked asked, proving how little he knew about the case.

Julia was about to explain, but Jessie pulled her own plastic bag containing her phone out of her pocket. She pressed a couple of buttons before a highly exposed and slightly blurry picture filled the frame. She pinched the screen and zoomed in on the shiny red writing on the sugar packets. Barker gulped and looked up at Julia.

"It's blood," Jessie whispered. "*Human* blood."

"'*Julia did it*,'" Barker whispered, tugging at his shirt collar. "That might explain a few things. Julia, you need to promise me that you're going to stay out of this investigation. You're still a suspect until they say otherwise. They're going to do everything they can to work around the evidence to make it fit their story. I should know, I work for them."

"I promise," Julia said as she stuffed her hands into her dressing gown. "I honestly just want to go home."

Barker kissed Julia gently on the forehead as he ruffled Jessie's hair. She batted his hand and ducked out of the way with a scowl. Julia chuckled, glad to see things going back to normal.

"I need to get to work," Barker said. "Somebody stole Imogen Carter's favourite garden gnome. They've put me on the case."

"Ever the *exciting* life, *eh*, Detective?" Jessie mocked.

"Watch your tongue, young lady," Barker said with a wink. "I could always go in there and fix it up so they charge you. I *know* people."

Espresso and Evil

"Bite me."

Julia laughed, kissed Barker one more time and turned to watch him walk into the station. When they were alone, Julia let out a sigh of relief.

"Your fingers were crossed in your pocket when you made that promise, weren't they?" Jessie asked flatly.

"No," Julia said as she quickly uncrossed her fingers. "But somebody has gone to great trouble to try and frame me for murder, and I'll be damned if I sit back and let them get away with it. Security footage or not, I need to clear my name before the mud sticks."

"Mine too," Jessie said with a firm nod.

Julia was about to tell Jessie to stay out of things, but she closed her mouth. She would be a hypocrite if she broke her false promise to Barker while also forcing Jessie to make the same promise. As she linked her arms through her young lodger's, she realised they were far more alike than either of them probably recognised.

***

JULIA AND JESSIE WALKED INTO THE heart of the village arm in arm. Her chest tightened when she spotted her café. Blue and white crime scene tape circled the small building, a forensics team swarming in and out like flies. She thought about them touching all of her baking things, and her heart hurt a little.

"I don't mind going to prison," Jessie said as she pulled away from Julia and clenched both of her fists. "I reckon I could take out *at least* three of them before they call for back-up."

Julia rested her hand on Jessie's to let her know she appreciated the gesture but she would rather they both stay as far away from the police station as they could until they were handing over the real murderer.

Turning away from her café, she looked in the direction of Happy Bean, which had similar men in white costumes combing over the scene. Her mind flashed back to Anthony Kennedy lying on the floor in his coffee shop. Despite everything that had happened, it upset Julia to think a man had needlessly died, especially one she had known for so long. She thought back to the way he had looked at her on the village green the day before, with his glowing orange tan and porcelain white teeth, devoid of any real emotion. It wasn't so different from the look she had seen on his dead face.

Espresso and Evil

Julia linked arms with Jessie and they set off. The thought of climbing into bed, even if she knew she wouldn't be able to sleep, was all that motivated her. She knew Anthony's untimely death wasn't going to be her café's saviour. Like most corporate beasts, another head always grew back when you cut off the first, and the second was usually much, much worse.

"Is that Dot?" Jessie asked, stopping in her tracks and looking at the village hall next to St. Peter's Church.

Julia shielded her eyes from the sun and squinted in the direction Jessie was looking. Her heart sank when she saw her gran, with a group of the other elderly villagers, marching towards her café with new t-shirts and protest signs.

"*Free Julia*!" Dot bellowed down the megaphone in the direction of the bewildered forensics team. "You can *try* and lock me up, and you can *throw* away the key, but we will not settle until she is *released*!"

"Maybe we should just leave her," Jessie whispered, holding Julia back. "It's too funny to spoil."

Julia considered it for a moment but shook her head. She looked down at her pyjamas and slippers, realising how silly she must look walking around the village.

"*What do we want?*" Dot cried.

"To free Julia!" the gang replied.

"*When do we want it?*"

The girls looked at each other, unsure of what the correct response was.

"*Now!*" Dot replied for them, pursing her lips and frowning heavily at her group. "*We want it now! Unleash* my granddaughter from your *evil* clutches or else I will – *Julia?*"

Julia smiled awkwardly as she walked forward. Dot, as well as the rest of the protesters, stared at her with bewilderment, as though she was walking on water, or had just risen from the dead. Dot immediately dropped her megaphone and pulled Julia into a suffocating hug.

"I'm fine, Gran," Julia gasped through the grip. "We're fine."

"Oh, *Julia!*" Dot cried into her ear. "We've been fearing the worst! Shilpa called and told us what Barker said about you being arrested for *murder*! I was on the phone first thing to the printers to get new t-shirts."

Dot tugged proudly at her t-shirt, which spelled out '*FREE JULIA*' in giant letters.

Espresso and Evil

"I couldn't bear the thought of you locked up in there," Amy Clark exclaimed as she pulled open her pale pink cardigan to reveal her t-shirt. "*I* should know what it's like."

"You robbed banks, Amy, you didn't bump off coffee shop owners," Emily Burns whispered, making Amy Clark nod meekly and pull her fluffy cardigan back across her chest. "It's good to see you back, Julia. Are those pyjamas?"

"It's a long story," Julia said, glancing through the window of her café as a man in a white suit swabbed her cake stand. "I'm sorry you wasted money on new t-shirts."

"No money wasted!" Dot announced with a grin. "I got them for free at the print shop on Mulberry Lane! Mr Shufflebottom was more than happy to accommodate our needs."

"You *did* blackmail him," Amy whispered, lifting a finger as she stepped forward.

"I *simply* said if he didn't do them, I would reveal his secret," Dot said with a shake of her perm as she glanced over her shoulder at Amy. "Do you have to be such a little snitch, Amy? I thought shacking up with the other criminals in cellblock H for a twenty stretch would have taught you better!"

"What secret?" Jessie asked.

"Oh, I didn't know one," Dot said with a smirk as she leaned into Jessie's ear. "But between you and me, *most* people have one, so it's a good tactic to use, kid." Dot winked and pinched Jessie's cheek. "He started blabbering about his gambling addiction before I had even finished my sentence. Worked a *treat*!"

Julia didn't know whether she should be flattered or horrified at the lengths her gran had gone to for the sake of protesting her arrest. She knew Dot cared, but part of her knew she was enjoying stirring the troops and protesting something. Dot's arrest had no doubt lit a rebellious fire under her feet. Julia made a mental note to make a tiramisu for Mr Shufflebottom, which she remembered was his favourite after sitting next to him in The Comfy Corner restaurant for Dot's birthday dinner last year.

"Well, I've had enough murder, blackmail, and extortion for one day," Julia said, another yawn escaping her lips before she could stop it. "I appreciate the effort, Gran, but you can put your feet up until the next worthy cause passes you by."

"*Nonsense!*" Dot cried as she unclipped her handbag and pulled out a black marker pen. "I'll just *change* them! There's more work to be done."

Espresso and Evil

Dot ripped open Amy's cardigan, crossed out *'FREE'* and scribbled *'IS INNOCENT'* under *'JULIA'*. Julia stepped forward to object, but Amy shook her head to let her know it was probably best to let Dot do what she wanted. Leaving her to finish correcting the group's t-shirts, Julia walked past her Ford Anglia, which was still parked where she had left it the night before. She realised it probably wasn't wise to try driving home on the little sleep she had had. For the second time that day, they set off back towards their cottage.

When they reached Happy Bean, she was surprised to see a woman with messy caramel hair laying a bouquet of pink lilies outside the coffee shop. Julia stopped in her tracks, her stomach knotting tightly. The woman wiped away a tear from her raw eyes with a sodden tissue before standing up. She too stopped in her tracks when she saw Julia, and to Julia's surprise, her top lip snarled and her nostrils flared. She looked as though she was going to say something, but she pushed through them and marched across the village, her head low and her hands tucked into her jacket pockets.

"I think she works at the hospital with Sue," Julia whispered to herself as she looked down at the flowers. "Word really does get around. She thinks

I'm guilty."

"Forget her," Jessie mumbled, dragging Julia away from the flowers. "What other people think of you is none of your business."

"That's very wise, Jessie."

"Read it on a sticker on a bus once," she said casually. "C'mon, Dolly and Dom might slip into a coma if we don't go home soon."

As they walked up the village lane, Julia couldn't shake the way the woman had looked at her. It didn't matter that she had been released from questioning for the time being, she knew the news of her arrest at the murder scene would be spreading around the village like wildfire. It didn't matter that she was innocent, the blame would be attached to her until the real culprit was discovered. Julia owed it to herself and Jessie to be the one to clear their names, no matter what it took.

She unlocked the door of her cottage and walked inside, glad to be home. Mowgli trotted out from the kitchen and circled her feet to let her know she was late putting his breakfast down. She peeped her head into the sitting room, where Dolly and Dom were still fast asleep exactly as they had been when they had left them the night before.

Jessie clapped her hands together, causing the

Espresso and Evil

twins to dart up, dribble on their cheeks, their blonde hair sticking up in every direction, and their eyes half-closed as though they hadn't had any sleep at all.

"What's for breakfast?" they asked in unison as they squinted at Jessie and Julia, none the wiser to what had happened.

Julia chuckled to herself and walked through to the kitchen. She fed Mowgli, made four peppermint and liquorice teas, and got to work making four full English breakfasts. She had been kidding herself that she was going to be able to sleep; she had far too much to think about.

CHAPTER 5

Mondays in Julia's café were always the quietest. Julia almost decided not to open, especially considering what had happened over the weekend. It had been Jessie who had convinced her that she should open, and as it turned out, they ended up taking record sales for a Monday. She knew it was because people wanted to get a look at the woman who killed Anthony

Espresso and Evil

Kennedy, but she was surprised by how little she cared about that. The till rang out all day, and that's all that mattered at the moment. Every extra penny prolonged her café's lifespan.

When she finally closed the café, she pulled the cottage pie she had prepared that morning out of the fridge, along with a strawberry pavlova she had managed to bake in one of the few quiet spells during the day.

After sending Jessie home, Julia drove across the village to Anthony Kennedy's cottage. She pulled up outside and yanked up the handbrake as she stared at his beautiful house. He had lived there for as long as Julia had known him, but it had undergone many transformations in that time. It was one of the bigger cottages in the village, with a beautifully presented garden in the front, and a large glass conservatory in the back. Grabbing the food from the back seat, she checked her reflection in the mirror, which looked considerably better after a good night of sleep and a nice hot shower. She could almost convince the world that everything was fine.

Julia wasn't sure how her visit was going to be received by Anthony's wife and son. Despite not having done anything wrong, she knew gossiping was intertwined with Peridale's DNA. Taking a deep breath, she unclipped the white gate and walked slowly down the garden path, hoping the rumour mill hadn't reached this far out yet. Balancing the cottage pie and strawberry pavlova in one hand, she pressed the doorbell. It rang out through the house, and she was surprised when the door opened almost instantly, giving Julia no time to second-guess her visit.

"*Julia?*" Rosemary Kennedy exclaimed, dressed as though she had just been about to go out. "What a surprise!"

Julia was glad Rosemary didn't immediately attack her, but she was a little unsettled with how put together the woman looked, considering her husband had died only the day before. Gone was the Happy Bean barista uniform, to be replaced with a well-fitting pair of black jeans, which hugged her figure beautifully. She had paired it with an orange blouse, which was tucked into the waist of her jeans, hanging over a little. Her lips were stained with red lipstick, and her shoulder-length grey hair was neatly curled and tucked behind her diamond-studded ears. She might have been a woman in her mid-sixties, but she looked effortlessly stylish.

"I brought you a cottage pie," Julia said, offering forward the dish. "And a pavlova. I didn't think

Espresso and Evil

you'd want to be worrying about cooking today."

"Come in," Rosemary said, stepping to the side to let Julia into the cottage. "That's incredibly sweet of you. Come through to the kitchen."

Julia followed Rosemary down the impeccably decorated hallway to the glossy kitchen, which faced directly into the conservatory, which in turn looked over their beautiful garden, complete with a swimming pool. Julia had never seen so much natural light flooding into a house before, and yet it lacked an ounce of charm that the exterior would suggest it possessed.

"I hope you don't mind me showing up here," Julia said as she pushed the food onto the counter. "I know I'm probably the last person you want to see right now."

"Oh, not at all!" Rosemary said with a small laugh. "I know *you* didn't kill Anthony, my love."

The joviality of Rosemary's laughter disturbed Julia, but she was glad she wasn't placing the blame on her for suddenly becoming a widow.

Rosemary made them two cups of tea, which she took through to the conservatory. The sun was high in the clear July sky and beating down on the glass, not that Julia could feel it. A small air conditioning unit hummed quietly in the corner, keeping the glass room nice and cool. They sat in two wicker bucket chairs and stared out at the garden as they silently hugged their tea.

"How are you feeling?" Julia asked, breaking the awkward silence. "Stupid question, I know."

"Honestly?" Rosemary asked, inhaling deeply as she continued to look out at the garden. "I feel free."

Julia opened her mouth to speak, but she had no idea what to say. She stared at Rosemary, and free seemed like the perfect word to describe the content expression on her lightly make-up covered face. When Julia had seen Rosemary on Saturday ripping her apron off after denying her husband a kiss, she had looked like she had had the weight of the world on her shoulders. Julia's eyes wandered down to her fingers. Just as she had suspected, she was missing her left index finger acrylic nail. What was left behind looked painful and coarse, as though it had been ripped clean off. The only time Julia had ever endured acrylic nails was when she had been Sue's maid of honour. She had guilt-tripped Julia into believing she needed them to complete the wedding, so she reluctantly went along with it. The extensions had been so cumbersome and alien, she had felt completely incapacitated for the entire day. Not being used to them, she had banged them more than

Espresso and Evil

a couple of times and the pain was incomparable to anything she had ever experienced. She couldn't imagine how it would feel to have one ripped off.

"I suppose you know I was the one to find Anthony's body," Julia started, pausing to check Rosemary was even listening beneath her calm exterior. "Somebody planted a bottle of poison in my café, and they left a message there, pinning the murder on me."

"Arsenic poisoning," Rosemary mumbled, her brows twitching, her expression still vacant. "That's what the police are saying. They're still running tests."

"Do you have any idea who would want to frame me for Anthony's murder?" Julia asked, edging forward in her seat, her heart beating as she got straight to the point of her visit. "I know me and Anthony didn't seem like the best of friends. He was trying to destroy my business after all, but I would never resort to *that*. I know he didn't like me, but I knew him too long to truly hate him *that* much."

"You're right," Rosemary said, suddenly turning to face Julia. "He didn't like you. He didn't like anyone. All he liked was himself, and money. *Look* at that swimming pool. I can count on one hand how many times he used it, but he made sure to swindle as many people as he could to pay for it. I hope the next people who buy this place fill it with cement."

"You're selling the cottage?"

"Of course," Rosemary said with a soft chuckle. "Just look at this place. It's devoid of any personality. It's him all over. Any personality this place had when we moved in, he stripped it away and replaced it with glass and metal."

Julia looked down at the white marble tiles, not wanting Rosemary to see how uncomfortable she looked. She was talking as though she had just divorced him, instead of what had really happened. Julia wondered if she was in denial. If she was, she couldn't blame her. What unsettled Julia the most was how lucid and present she looked.

"Will you stay in Peridale?" Julia asked.

"Perhaps," she said with a shrug. "Maybe I'll move somewhere new. Somewhere where I can *be* somebody new."

Footsteps signalled the arrival of Gareth, their son. He walked into the conservatory as though he was about to say something but he bit his tongue when he saw Julia.

"*Oh*," he said, his cheeks burning red. "Hello."

"Hello, Gareth," Julia said. "How are you feeling?"

Espresso and Evil

The teenager shrugged, and even though he looked a little less relieved than his mother, he didn't look particularly distraught either. Julia suddenly remembered his presence at the protest meeting at the village hall, and wondered what could have led him to being there.

"Dad's business partner is outside," Gareth said, looking past Julia to his mum. "He's talking to that guy from the station."

"He's early," Rosemary said, grabbing a photo frame from the window ledge to check her reflection. "Thanks for the cottage pie, Julia. I'm eating out tonight, but I'm sure Gareth will enjoy it."

Gareth shrugged and stuffed his hands into his pockets. Rosemary sprung up like a woman half her age. Julia couldn't be sure, but she was sure Rosemary looked like she was about to go on a date.

Julia followed Rosemary down the hallway and back to the front door, feeling none the wiser as to who could have wanted to frame her for murder. She had been racking her brain all day in the café trying to think of people she had wronged, but she couldn't think of any rivalry that would result in a murder charge. The only person she could think of who might have gone to those extremes was the man who was now lying on a slab in the morgue.

Rosemary grabbed her handbag from the bannister, unclipped it, and pulled out a small bottle of perfume. After dousing herself in the sweet, floral scent, she checked that she didn't have lipstick on her teeth in the hallway mirror, slid her feet into simple black heels, and opened the door.

When Julia saw Barker standing at the bottom of the garden talking to another man, the wind knocked out of her sails, and the rug pulled from under her feet. She was aware that Rosemary was saying something to her, but she couldn't hear a thing other than the intense beating of her heart. All she could do was stare, until Anthony's business partner turned to face her, as though in slow motion. She hadn't seen that smug smirk in so long, but she recognised it in an instant.

"Jerrad, you're early," Rosemary said as she walked down the path. "Julia, are you coming?"

"I thought I'd surprise you," the man said with a leer as he pushed his suit jacket away to stuff his hands into his trouser pockets. "Hello, *Julia*. It's been a while."

Julia swallowed and walked forward, her legs like jelly. She met Barker's eyes, and he looked at her with a confused smile. She tried to smile back, but

Espresso and Evil

she wasn't sure her lips moved beyond a shivery twitch.

Jerrad was thinner and his hair looked different, but there was no denying who she was looking at. She realised she hadn't imagined things when she thought she had seen him talking with Anthony outside the coffee shop on Saturday afternoon.

"You know each other?" Rosemary asked, stopping in front of Julia and looking curiously down at her from her heel-elevated height. "It's a small world, isn't it?"

"You could say that," he said, his smirk growing wider and wider. "She's my wife."

"*Ex*-wife," Julia blurted out, her blank mind reacting on impulse rather than thought.

"I think you need to speak to your lawyer, darlin'," Jerrad said, barely able to contain his pleasure as he reached forward to unclip the gate for Rosemary. "I never signed the papers. We're still married. Are you ready, Rosemary?"

Julia watched as Rosemary followed Jerrad towards a flashy sports car she didn't recognise. He opened the door for her, but he wasn't able to take his dark stare off Julia. Looking as though she was just as flummoxed, Rosemary craned her neck to stare back at Julia as Jerrad practically forced her into the car. Before he climbed in himself, he sent her a final wink, which turned her entire body to stone. It wasn't until the car sped away and vanished into the countryside that she could even bring herself to look at Barker.

"I can explain," she mumbled feebly.

Barker looked as though he was going to speak, but no words left his lips. He pinched between his brows, exhaled heavily, and turned with a shake of his head, as though he couldn't look at Julia; he looked disgusted. He pulled his keys from his pocket, jumped into his car, and sped in the opposite direction without a second look at Julia.

She didn't know what to say, or what to feel. Her past and her present had just collided so heavily, she couldn't imagine how there could possibly be any future.

"How long do I cook this thing for?" Gareth called through the still open front door.

Julia didn't realise she was crying until she wiped the tears away. She turned and walked back inside to help Gareth cook the cottage pie.

CHAPTER 6

"You *silly* girl," Dot said as she looked over the paperwork in her hand. "You should have checked to make sure everything was final!"

"I know," Julia mumbled, unable to look at the letter her lawyer had sent to her.

"Just because you signed the papers, it doesn't mean you're divorced," Dot said as she tossed the

Agatha Frost

paper onto her dining room table. "Didn't your lawyer explain that to you?"

"I know that now," Julia said, trying not to get frustrated with her gran. "It's not like I've been divorced before. Jerrad had been badgering me so much through my lawyer, I just thought he'd already signed his half. I dragged my heels for so long before signing them."

"When did you sign them?" Dot asked.

"March," Julia mumbled pathetically. "They were on my kitchen counter for months before I could even open them."

"It's only July!" Dot cried. "Oh, Julia. You silly, *silly* girl. It needs to go before a judge before it's official, and that's only if you've both signed the agreement." Dot was just echoing what the lawyer had told her on the phone the night before. "Eat your dinner. You can't go hungry."

Julia looked down at the lamb chops and mash, but she wasn't hungry. She had been pushing the food around the plate, as had Sue, who looked as upset as Julia at everything that had happened. Julia tried to smile at her sister, to reassure her that she was fine, but she knew her eyes betrayed her.

"I can hit him," Jessie remarked suddenly after pushing her plate away. "Or even better, I'll get Billy

Espresso and Evil

to do it."

"What good will that do?" Sue asked with a shake of her head as her hands rested on her bump. "Violence doesn't solve anything."

"It will make me feel better," Jessie mumbled. "And a black eye might make Julia feel better."

Julia wasn't sure what would make her feel better. She picked up her phone and called Barker for what felt like the hundredth time that day. It had been an hour since his phone had stopped ringing, now going straight through to his voicemail. Julia had tried to leave a message more than once, but she knew nothing she could say would fix the mess she had caused.

"There's still a murderer out there," Dot said softly, reaching out to touch Julia's hand. "That should keep your mind off things."

"Is that supposed to cheer her up?" Sue asked with a laugh. "Half of the village think Julia did it, and the other half think Jessie did it, and the rest think both of them did it together."

"You can't have more than two halves," Jessie corrected her with a roll of her eyes. "That baby has pickled your already tiny brain."

Sue sat up in her chair, clearly offended. Julia let out a small laugh. It was the first time she had felt an emotion all day that wasn't dread. Sue dropped her stern expression and joined in the laughing.

"Leave my little lime out of things," Sue said with a rub of her stomach.

"I don't like limes," Dot mumbled thoughtfully. "Lemons, on the other hand, they're a real fruit. They taste delicious and are great for polishing silverware."

"They taste the same," Jessie fired across the table. "Both sour."

A heated debate about the difference between lemons and limes started across the table, but Julia had already tuned out. She was glad they were talking about something other than her divorce, or lack of one. She picked up the letter and read over the legal jargon that her lawyer had sent special delivery overnight, just confirming what he had told her on the phone.

When the debate died down, neither side having won, Julia helped Dot clear away the dishes, while Sue and Jessie went through to the sitting room where the café's leftover cakes were waiting for them.

"I think Rosemary is dating Jerrad," Julia thought aloud as she scraped her dinner into the bin. "She's twenty years older than him."

"Men are fickle," Dot replied as she filled the

Espresso and Evil

sink with water and washing up liquid. "One minute they want someone younger because they feel old, and then they want someone older because they realise twenty-year-old girls have empty heads and nothing in common. What did Rosemary have to say for herself?"

"Nothing much," Julia said as she closed the bin and placed her plate on the pile of others. "She didn't seem to care that her husband was dead. If she had suspected me of actually killing him, I'm sure she would have thanked me."

"I don't blame her," Dot mumbled as she snapped on her pink rubber gloves. "Your father and Anthony were cut from the same cloth. Both selfish, money-obsessed fools. If they can't throw money at something, they're not interested."

Julia thought about the five hundred pounds still sitting in her biscuit tin. She knew her father's vision was clouded by money, but she knew he wasn't as bad as Anthony had been.

"Did you know Anthony's mum?" Julia asked.

"I still do," Dot said as she put the first plate on the draining board. "Not that I've seen Barb in a while. She doesn't get down from the nursing home that often. We used to be quite close. Brian and Anthony were the best of friends from being knee

Agatha Frost

high, right up until that nasty business with Anthony taking your father's share of their company. I didn't speak to Barb again after that, just on principle. I might not be your father's biggest fan, but I have my integrity."

"I should speak to her," Julia said, almost to herself. "She might know something useful."

"I doubt it," Dot said as she added the second dish to the draining board. "Her and Anthony were never close. She once told me she looked for the mark of the devil on his forehead when he was sleeping. But, if you want to talk to her, we'll go now."

Dot snapped off her rubber gloves and tossed them on the side, leaving the rest of the dishes for later.

"Now?" Julia asked as Dot grabbed her coat from under the stairs. "I don't think it's a good time."

"No time like the present!" she announced as she pulled on her beige coat. "It will keep your mind busy. *Girls*, we're going out. We'll be back in a jiffy. Don't touch my good biscuits!"

Julia almost protested, but her gran was right. She needed something to take her mind off things, and talking to Anthony's mother provided that

Espresso and Evil

distraction, if only temporarily.

***

OAKWOOD NURSING HOME SAT ON THE outskirts of Peridale, surrounded by acres of sprawling countryside and no other signs of life for miles. They took a small winding lane up to the old manor house, which dated back to the early 19th century, according to Dot. It looked like a luxury hotel, rather than a place where the elderly would spend their twilight years.

"If I start dribbling and you need to put me in a home, I'd like it to be this one," Dot whispered as she looked up at the canopy of oak tree leaves above them. "Not that *you'd* ever be able to afford it."

Julia's tyres crunched against the gravel as she followed the signs for guest parking, which took her around the back of the building. When they parked next to the half a dozen other cars, they walked back to the entrance, pausing to stare at the beautiful stone water feature directly in front of the grand doors.

Once inside, the scent of flowers hit them immediately. They walked along the marble floor of the grand entrance hall towards a reception desk, which was filled with fresh, white lilies.

"*This* is the life!" Dot exclaimed excitedly into Julia's ear. "Luxury at its finest! Ol' Barb has done alright for herself here."

Julia approached the reception desk while her gran marvelled at the grand chandelier glittering above. Applying her friendliest smile, Julia waited until the well-dressed young nurse behind the reception desk looked up from a copy of *Sense and Sensibility*. She waited until she finished the page she was reading, before turning and looking up with a smile so wide, it looked too bright to be anything but genuine.

"Hello," she cooed softly. "Welcome to Oakwood Nursing Home. How can I help you today?"

"We want to speak with Barb," Julia said, realising she didn't even know the woman's surname "Barb Kennedy?"

"Barbara?" the nurse asked with a nod. "We have a *Barbara* here."

"She went by Barb in my day," Dot mumbled out of the corner of her mouth. "Probably too common for lady muck now."

"Are you on her approved visiting list?" the nurse asked, her smile still beaming. "Is she

Espresso and Evil

expecting you?"

"What is this?" Dot asked, slapping her hands on the desk. *"Prison?"*

The nurse's smile faltered for the first time as she recoiled her head. Her smile bounced back in a second before she rolled across the marble floor in her chair to the computer.

"They're going to ask us to take our shoes off and send us through scanners next," Dot whispered. *"Ridiculous!"*

"Rosemary?" the nurse asked, looking up at them.

"Yes, that's me," Dot said quickly, pushing Julia out of the way, plastering a smile on her face. "*I* am Rosemary."

"Barbara wasn't expecting you until tomorrow, but I'm sure she won't mind the early visit," the nurse said as she typed away at her keyboard. "And *you* are?"

"This is my daughter," Dot said before Julia could answer.

"Gareth?" the nurse asked, her brows arching as she stared suspiciously at Dot.

"It's short for *Garethina*," Dot blurted out, stamping on Julia's foot to let her know not to say a word. "It's a very common name in Germany."

"You're German?"

"Fräulein uske-be clair!" Dot chanted enthusiastically. "May we enter your *fine* establishment now?"

"Barbara is in the television room enjoying a cup of tea," the nurse said as she pressed a button under the desk, which buzzed and unlocked the nearest door. "Through there, follow it down to the bottom, and take the first right."

"I'm sure we'll find it," Dot mumbled, slipping her hand through Julia's and dragging her to the door, before pausing and turning back to the nurse. "You're only a receptionist, you know. You're not holding the keys to heaven."

With that, Dot tugged Julia through the door before the young woman could reply. Julia didn't need to see her face to know she had probably lost her bright smile.

"I didn't know you spoke German," Julia whispered as she pulled her hand free.

"I don't," Dot said with a shrug. "That was complete nonsense, but it sounded good, didn't it? You've got to think on your toes, Julia! Honestly, I don't know *how* you've cracked so many murder cases! I'll chalk this one down to you having a lot on your mind. *Ah*, here we go! The television room."

Espresso and Evil

From what Julia knew of nursing homes, the television room was usually a dark and depressing space were the silent elderly faced a tiny, ancient TV, while watching *Cash in the Attic*, *Songs of Praise*, and *Countdown* in between bouts of medication. What she hadn't been expecting was an airy, open room, lined with bookshelves, and filled with chatter and laughter. Comfy chairs cluttered the room, facing in every direction other than the TV, which appeared to be there purely for background noise. A group of men were gathered around a pool table in the middle of the room, taking it in turns to pot the ball, while the rest of the residents looked on, chatting in between pots and cheering when a ball made its way into a pocket.

"There she is," Dot whispered, marching forward to a group of women who were sat in a cluster of armchairs in the corner of the room as they played a game of chess.

"You're *cheating*, Barb!" one of the women exclaimed. "You're *far* too good at this!"

"Just because I'm about to win, it doesn't mean I'm cheating," Barb replied with a wicked grin. "*Checkmate!*"

The other woman sat back in her chair and sighed, while Barb sat back and crossed one tan-tight covered leg over the other, looking pleased with herself. Julia wasn't sure if she had been expecting a frail old woman, but that's not what Barb was. Just like her gran, she looked to be in her eighties, and also like her gran, didn't look like she was ready to slow down and accept old age just yet. She was wearing a white and pink floral blouse, and her white hair, which looked impossibly long, was swept up into a giant bun that sat neatly on the top of her head, not a single hair out of place.

"*Dorothy?*" Barb called out. "Is that *you?*"

"It is, Barb," Dot said. "You're looking well."

"As are you," Barb said through a strained smile. "Ladies, excuse me."

Barb got out of her low armchair with ease, nodding to the women in her group as she did. She hooked her arm through Dot's and led her through open French doors and into the never-ending garden.

"I didn't realise Oakwood was taking applications," Barb said as Julia lingered behind. "It's good to see you, old friend."

"I'm just here visiting," Dot said. "Well, we're here to see you, actually. This is my granddaughter, Julia."

Barb sat on a low wall overlooking the saturated

Espresso and Evil

vegetation ahead of them, its hue impossibly vivid. She smiled her recognition at Julia, before narrowing her eyes, and snapping her fingers together.

"Brian's daughter?" she asked, looking Julia up and down. "I haven't seen you since you were in nappies! How's your mum?"

"Dead," Julia answered.

"Of course," Barb mumbled, tapping her chin with her finger before it drifted up to her temple. "The memory fades with age. I'm sorry, dear. I didn't mean any offence. What's the reason for your visit today? I'd like to say it was to rebuild old bridges, but I know you don't do anything for nothing, Dorothy."

"It's *Dot*, now," she corrected her. "As you are now Barbara."

"We all change, Dorothy," she said, ignoring her gran's correction. "You don't look a day over eighty-nine!"

"I'm only eighty-*three*," Dot seethed through pursed lips. "You know I'm five years younger than you."

"Ah, yes," Barb said, tapping her temple once more. "The memory."

Dot glanced at Julia out of the corner of her eye, giving her the impression it was nothing to do with her memory, and more to do with this being how Barb was.

"I assume you've heard?" Dot asked.

"About my son's murder?" she replied coolly. "Of course. News travels fast in this village."

"You don't seem upset," Dot said bluntly. "He was your son."

"You know we weren't close," she said with a wave of her hand. "One reluctant flying visit every Friday for ten years doesn't constitute a close relationship. He looked at his watch the entire time. I was a chore to him. Nothing more, nothing less."

Julia was struck by the woman's coldness, despite delivering everything with a sweet smile. She couldn't imagine her gran being so callous if her own son died, no matter how strained their relationship was. Julia wasn't a mother, so maybe she didn't understand the complexities that came with it, but she had Jessie, and no matter how far apart they might drift, they were connected forever, and if anything ever happened to Jessie, Julia wouldn't be able to brush it off as something as trivial as a change in the weather.

"The thing is, Barb, somebody is trying to frame my granddaughter for your son's murder," Dot said, glancing uncomfortably at Julia. "Naturally, she

Espresso and Evil

didn't do it, but she found the body, and there is some rather - let's say - *incriminating*, evidence."

"Okay?" Barb replied, glancing back at the television room as though she wanted nothing more than to return to her game of chess. "How can I help?"

"We were just wondering if you knew if Anthony had any enemies," Julia asked, speaking up for the first time. "I just want to piece things together so I can clear my name."

Barb leaned forward and looked at Julia, her lips twisting as though she was containing a laugh. She held it back for a second before letting it burst free as she looked between the two of them.

"How long have you got?" Barb asked with a chuckle. "My son's favourite hobby was making enemies. From the time he first realised that money equalled power he was out for himself. He was a lovely baby, you know. He first stole from my purse when he was four. Took a shilling and six pence and used it to con one of his friends out of their Slinky. Sold it on to another for half a crown. Sometimes, I wonder if there was anything I could have done, but some children just come out wrong."

That sounded like the Anthony Julia knew. Even when she had been a child, he would dig through the toys her mother would buy her from car boot sales to see if any of them were rare or worth a penny or two.

"We were looking for some specific names," Julia asked.

"Ask your father," Barb snapped, her smile dropping. "How did you even get in here anyway? Neither of you is on my list."

Barb looked like she was going to continue with her rant, but a young nurse with long dark hair appeared behind them, holding a silver tray with a cup of pills and a glass of water.

"*Ah!* Yelena!" Barb exclaimed, clapping her hands together. "Just in time. Dot, it was nice catching up. Julia, good seeing you again. I must go and take my pills. You know what it's like at this age."

"I didn't want to interrupt," Yelena said, her accent clearly Eastern European. "But you said –"

"You're not interrupting anything," Dot mumbled as she scratched the side of her head, her brows high up her forehead. "See you around, Barb."

With that, she pushed off the wall and walked back into the television room, followed by Yelena who smiled meekly at Dot and Julia over her

Espresso and Evil

shoulder. Julia looked on in disbelief as Barb took her pills, shooed Yelena away, and started another game of chess. Just like Rosemary, she was totally unfazed. She wondered if this was a natural reaction she was going to receive from anybody close to Anthony.

"Imagine being that evil that your own mother doesn't mourn your death," Dot said. "Let's get out of here. I can feel them trying to absorb your youth like a nicotine patch."

They hurried back through the television room, back down the corridor, and into the entrance hall. The receptionist jumped up and ran forward, clutching something in her hands.

"Take a brochure?" she asked Dot with a bright smile. "We offer competitive rates."

"Thank you," Dot said, taking the thick, green volume before walking towards the exit and dumping it straight into the small bin next to the door. "I take it back, Julia. If I ever need putting in one of these places, take me to the fields and shoot me like a horse with a broken leg. Did you see how cheery they all were? It's practically sickening!"

Before Julia could reply, her heart stopped when she saw Barker's familiar car drive past, its tyres crunching on the gravel. Julia waited for him to park

Agatha Frost

and make his way around to the front. When he saw her, he looked surprised that she was there. He stopped in his tracks and looked over his shoulder as though he was deciding if he should turn around. To her relief, he didn't, and he pressed forward.

"I'll wait in the car," Dot whispered as she slipped the keys from Julia's pocket. "*Barker.*"

"Dot," he replied with a curt nod. "*Julia.*"

"Barker," Julia said, hating how they suddenly felt like strangers again. "How are you?"

"I'm fine," he said, his eyes vacant and slightly red. "You?"

Julia almost responded with an automated answer, but her heart and mind were racing, trying to overtake the other.

"I'm sorry," she said. "I was going to tell you."

Barker gulped and looked down at the car keys in his hand. For a moment, she thought he might start crying, or even shout at her, but he looked up, his expression blank. She would have preferred anger over indifference.

"Why are you here?" he asked her.

"Visiting an old friend of Dot's," Julia said, hating that she was telling a lie to cover the fact she had lied about her promise not to investigate. "You?"

"Smashed window," he said. "Some kids from

Espresso and Evil

the Fern Moore Estate. Nothing too serious. I should get inside. They're expecting me."

Julia nodded and stepped to the side, staring at him and willed him to look back at her with the kind eyes she had come to know and love.

"I *really* am sorry," Julia called after him before he opened the door. "I honestly thought we were divorced."

Barker dropped his head again, before turning and looking at her. She knew that wasn't the point. She knew she should have told him either way. She caught a glimpse of the kindness she loved, and it sent her heart racing rapidly. No sooner had it returned did it vanish again.

"I just want you to be happy, Julia," he said heavily, dropping his eyes once more. "I need some space to think."

Julia nodded her understanding, even if she didn't want to. She wanted nothing more than to grab Barker and hold him until everything was fine again, but she wasn't entirely sure that he wouldn't push her away in an instant.

"Okay," was all she could think to say.

Barker half-smiled before pulling on the door and slipping into the nursing home. When he vanished, she grabbed fistfuls of her hair in frustration as she stared up hopelessly at the sky.

"Jessie sent you a text message," Dot said, Julia's phone in her hand as she climbed into her car. "She's back at your cottage. How are things?"

"Not good," Julia said before twisting the key in the ignition and reversing so quickly her wheels spun hopelessly against the gravel. "But can you blame him?"

Julia didn't realise she was driving fast until she pulled up outside her gran's cottage minutes after leaving the nursing home. Dot invited her in for some tea, but Julia declined, just wanting to be at home. She sped up to her cottage and walked through the unlocked door. She headed into the kitchen, surprised to see Jessie and Billy.

"*Oh*," Julia said. "Am I interrupting something?"

"Billy was just leaving," Jessie said through gritted teeth. "Weren't you, Billy?"

"Alright, alright," he said, backing away with his hands in the air. "Call me, yeah, babe?"

"I'm not your '*babe*'," Jessie said with a roll of her eyes. "Just clear off, will you?"

Billy winked at Jessie before doubling back and leaving the way Julia had just arrived. When they were alone, Julia went straight for the kettle and made herself and Jessie a cup of peppermint and

Espresso and Evil

liquorice tea.

"Are you okay?" Jessie asked softly, a hand resting on her shoulder. "He just turned up here. I didn't invite him."

"I'm fine," Julia lied, forcing back the tears and injecting a smile into her voice. "It's your home too, Jessie. You can invite anyone you want here. Grab the ice cream from the freezer. We can eat it with a film. You can pick."

Julia took the two teas into the living room where Jessie was waiting with two spoons, an open tub of vanilla ice cream, and the *Breakfast at Tiffany's* DVD menu on the screen. Julia was touched.

"I know it's old and boring, but it's your favourite film," Jessie said meekly.

Julia sat next to Jessie, rested her head on her shoulder, grabbed a spoon, tucked into the ice cream, and pressed play on the film. Even if Barker wasn't there with her, she was going to try and enjoy her evening with three of her favourite people: Audrey Hepburn, George Peppard, and Jessie.

CHAPTER 7

Wednesday evenings had become one of Julia's favourite days of the week. It was the day Jessie spent at college studying towards her apprenticeship, and when she came home, she brought Dolly and Dom with her for dinner. Cooking for the three of them had become a routine Julia looked forward to because having a house full of teenagers was something she never

Espresso and Evil

thought she would experience. This Wednesday, however, there was a space at the table where Barker should have been. Julia had even set a place for him before she remembered.

If Dolly and Dom noticed the lack of Barker's presence, they didn't mention it. Julia wondered if Jessie had told them not to bring him up, but she wasn't sure they would remember not to if she had. It always amused Julia how much they attempted to probe Barker about his cases, and how he always tried his best to dodge their questioning, answering them as a politician would; by not answering them at all. If he had told them he was investigating the murder of a rainbow coloured elephant, they probably would have lapped it up.

"This casserole is top quality," Dolly mumbled through a mouthful of food, barely pausing for air. "Thanks, Ju."

"It's *Julia*," Jessie corrected her without missing a beat. "Ju-li-*a*."

"I like Ju more," Dom added, also barely pausing. "Rolls off the tongue. *Juuuuuuu.*"

"Ju-Ju," Dolly added. "Sounds like chew-chew."

Jessie rolled her eyes, but Julia chortled. Most of the time, the twins spoke their own language of childlike gibberish, but it distracted her, and she needed that. They made Jessie look completely adult in comparison, despite being the same age.

After dinner, Jessie helped Julia take the dishes through to the kitchen. It hadn't gone unnoticed to Julia that Jessie had glanced at Barker's empty space more than once.

"Did you invite him?" Jessie asked as she scraped the leftovers into the bin.

"He said he needed space," Julia said, trying to stay as calm as possible. "It's the least I can do."

"He'll come 'round," Jessie said, smiling at Julia hopefully in the dark reflection of the window. "He's not so bad."

Julia smiled back, but she wasn't as sure as Jessie. She had seen the hurt in his eyes, and she had caused that. She looked down as she filled the sink with water, hoping she could hold back the tears until she was alone. Why hadn't she just been honest with him from the start?

"Why is *he* even in Peridale?" Jessie asked. "I thought Jerrad lived in London?"

"I don't know," Julia said, not having given him much thought because of Barker consuming her thoughts. "I haven't seen him again."

"Happy Bean is back open," Jessie reminded her. "Do you think he's involved with that?"

Espresso and Evil

The thought had crossed Julia's mind, but she couldn't figure out why Jerrad was interested in investing in a small chain coffee shop in a village that barely featured on the map. Jerrad dealt with high-stakes property investment, which had helped him get very rich over the years.

"He looked different," Julia said. "Like it was him, but it wasn't him. He seemed thinner and taller, and he looked like he had more hair."

A knock at the door interrupted their conversation. Julia pulled her hands out of the soapy water and wiped them on a tea towel, leaving Jessie to take over. She popped her head into the dining room, where Dolly and Dom were thumb wrestling; neither of them seemed to be winning.

"Hello, Julia," her father said when she opened the door. "Are you busy?"

"I've just finished dinner," she replied, glancing over her shoulder to the kitchen and spotting Jessie craning her neck around the side of the fridge. "Is everything okay?"

"Everything's fine," he said, tucking his face into the high collar of his overcoat. "Do you want to come for a walk?"

Julia didn't question him. She swapped her slippers for her comfortable shoes, told Jessie she would be ten minutes, and followed her dad out of her garden and onto the winding lane. Instead of walking back towards the village, he walked up the lane towards Peridale Farm, which was the last stop before the village ended.

"It's a lovely night," he said quietly as he tucked his hands into his jacket pockets and looked up at the dark sky, the last streaks of the pink sunset lingering on the horizon. "I need to get out more. I miss a lot being cooped up in that old manor."

Julia bit her tongue. She almost reminded him that it had been his choice to marry a woman the same age as his eldest daughter and join her reclusive family, who lived in Peridale but had never been part of the community.

"How's Katie's father doing?" she asked, deciding it was better to continue with the small talk until he got to the point.

"He's as good as he can be," he said, sucking the cool night air through his teeth. "He's comfortable. Since that last stroke, he hasn't said a word, but Katie keeps trying. I think he knows she's there, but it's difficult for her."

Julia thought back to the time Katie's father, Vincent Wellington, had saved her life when she was being carried to her death by the murderer of Katie's

Espresso and Evil

brother. If it hadn't been for him pressing the emergency call button and waking everybody up, she would have followed Charles out of the window and down to her death.

"Your gran called," he said as a car passed them on the narrow lane, the headlights blinding her. "She told me about Anthony, but half the village had already called by that point. I think people put two and two together and guessed I might know something because we used to be in business together."

"You used to be more than that," Julia said, remembering what her gran had said about them being friends from childhood. "He was your best man."

"I was blind," he said, dropping his head. "I wasted my life working with that man, avoiding my problems."

A lump rose in Julia's throat. She thought about all the times she had sat by her gran's sitting room window waiting for her father to return from his many business trips. It hadn't taken her long, even as a child, to realise the gaps between the visits home were growing and the time spent at home was shrinking. Their relationship had never repaired beyond that point. Seeing him twice in one week felt unusual for Julia, but she appreciated the effort he was putting in. She knew it would have taken a lot for him to swallow his pride and knock on her door.

"Why did you come here, Dad?" Julia asked, stopping and leaning against the wall before they reached Peridale Farm. "It's not like you were passing by."

He laughed softly and joined her in leaning against the wall. He ran his fingers through his thick, blow-dried hair, which was styled similarly to how Anthony's had been, but brown and grey instead of yellow blonde.

"Your gran asked me about Anthony's enemies," he started, turning to look at her. "I apparently gave her the same answer as Barb. He wasn't on a lot of people's favourite's lists, mine included."

"Are you upset he was killed?"

He thought for a moment, looked up at the sky, and shrugged meekly with tight lips. Julia could tell that he was upset, which was more than she had seen from any of the man's family so far. She knew it meant something deep down that the best man at his wedding was now dead, even if they hadn't spoken in years.

"I wrote down a couple of names," he said, ignoring the question. He reached into his pocket

Espresso and Evil

and pulled out a small hand-written list, which was on thick Wellington monogrammed paper. "I know you're looking into it. I gave the same list to the police, just to be fair."

Julia looked over the names on the list, all of them belonging to men. She didn't recognise any of them.

"Do any of these men live in Peridale?" Julia asked, knowing how far an antique dealer's net could stretch.

"These two do," he said, pointing to the top two names on the list. "Timothy Edwards and Mike Andre. I called some of my old contacts and they were more than forthcoming with names. According to them, Anthony had stopped trying to be even a little honest in the last couple of months and had been conning every single person he came into contact with. There's definitely more, but this is a start."

"It's a good start," Julia said, pocketing the list. "Thank you. Who do you think killed him, Dad?"

He sucked the air through his teeth once more and looked dead ahead at the horizon as the sky completely faded to black. Julia could make out the lights lining the motorway in the distance as the cars whizzed up and down the lanes, but they were too far away to hear.

"He was a cold man," he said. "He'd been unfaithful to Rosemary for years, and I think she knew it."

Julia thought about how unbothered she had been, and the apparent date she had been on with Jerrad. Julia almost told her father that her estranged husband was in the village, but she realised they had only met a couple of times over the course of their twelve-year marriage.

"Do you know any of the women who were his mistresses?" Julia asked as they set off back to her cottage. "That might help."

"Not *just* women," he said, his brows darting high up his lined forehead. "Anthony was never fussy when it came to *that*. The last I heard, he was seeing a woman from the hospital, but that was when we were still on speaking terms."

Julia almost dismissed the information because it had been so long ago, but she suddenly remembered seeing the woman laying flowers at the coffee shop and how she had been sure she had seen her at the hospital Sue worked at. Julia had been so tired, she had thought the woman was just blaming her with her eyes because of the gossip she had heard, but as she thought back, she could see the grief burning

Espresso and Evil

behind the woman's glassy gaze.

"I should be getting back," he said, pausing at Julia's gate before going any further. "Don't forget Sunday lunch at the manor. Have you asked Sue yet?"

"We'll come," Julia said, not wanting to admit she had completely forgotten about the lunch, or to ask Sue. The look of hopefulness in her father's eyes surprised her, and it made it impossible to refuse the invitation. "I promise."

He nodded and backed away, before turning and walking down the winding lane towards the village. Across the road, Julia noticed Emily twitching at her net curtains. Julia waved, which caused Emily to quickly retreat back into the safety of her living room.

"What did he have to say?" Jessie asked as she wiped her hands, the washing up completely finished. "Didn't want his money back, did he?"

"He came to give me information," Julia said, clutching the note to her chest before passing it to Jessie. "Recognise any of those names?"

She knew it was a long shot, and she didn't actually expect Jessie to know any of the men on the list, so she was shocked when the girl's eyes opened wide and she nodded her head.

"Mike Andre," she said with certainty. "He was a tutor at my college. Emigrated to Australia a couple of months ago. Who are these people?"

"Potential enemies of Anthony Kennedy," Julia said as she pinned the note to the fridge under a cat magnet. "People my dad thinks might have been conned enough to resort to murder. If Mike Andre left Peridale months before the murder, that only leaves one other name on his list in the village."

Julia pulled a pen from her kitchen's clutter drawer, pulled the cap off with her teeth, and circled '*Timothy Edwards*' until it was the only name she could see.

"It's a good start," she said, echoing what she had said to her dad.

"I'll grab the phonebook," Jessie said, already walking into the hallway. "I'll start ringing those other names to see if any of them were near Peridale this weekend."

Julia almost stopped her, but she let her return with the blue public directory phonebook. She knew all Jessie wanted to do was make herself useful, so if this were what she wanted to do, she would let her; it would keep her out of any real trouble.

While Jessie started ringing through the numbers in the dining room with Dolly and Dom,

Espresso and Evil

Julia took her mobile phone into the bathroom and called her sister.

"Sue? It's me. Do you know a woman who works at your hospital who might have been having an affair with Anthony Kennedy?"

CHAPTER 8

Peridale ran through Julia's veins. It was the village she had been born in, along with generations of her family for as long as anybody could remember. Even though she had been living back in Peridale for two years, Julia still felt like a fool for running off with a charming man to the big, bright city. It had taken two years back in her natural habitat to realise the lure of something

Espresso and Evil

entirely different than what she had always known was what had tempted her so strongly. Now that she was back where she belonged, nothing could make her leave again.

During their marriage, Jerrad had made his feeling on Peridale clear. He thought it was a backwards, dead-end village, where things went to die and ideas were stifled. What he had always failed to realise was that it was a buzzing community filled with life and laughter. Julia had never forgotten that.

Remembering this made it even stranger to look out of her café window and see Jerrad across the village green clearing a table outside Happy Bean. Since opening an hour ago, four different villagers had come in to tell Julia that Anthony's secret business partner was now running the coffee shop, which only confirmed her suspicions as to Jerrad's sudden appearance in the village. The question she couldn't stop asking herself was why? Why a coffee shop? Why in Peridale? Why now?

"We've run out of semi-skimmed milk," Jessie said as she poured the last of it into a latte for Roxy Carter, one of Julia's oldest friends from childhood, who was now a teacher at St. Peter's Primary School in the village.

"He looks different," Roxy said, tucking her

flame red hair behind her ears as she joined Julia in staring out of the window at Jerrad as he slowly wiped a table, no doubt to taunt Julia. "I know I only met him a couple of times, but he looks different."

"I know," Julia mumbled. "I can't figure out why."

"You don't still –"

"Have feelings for him?" Julia scoffed, the suggestion turning her stomach. "That's the *last* thing on my mind right now."

"*Milk!*" Jessie cried with a roll of her eyes as she tossed the empty carton in the bin and poured the steamed milk in with the espresso shot.

Julia took Roxy's money and handed over the latte, before taking a five-pound note from the petty cash and joining Roxy in walking out of the café.

"He's looking over," Roxy said, squinting into the sun as she sipped her hot latte. "*Mmmm*, you've trained that girl well, Julia. She knows how to make coffee."

"Jerrad doesn't even like coffee," Julia remembered aloud. "Why a coffee shop?"

"Even the dying towns have busy coffee shops," she said before taking another sip of her latte. "Although you know I'll always be loyal to you."

Espresso and Evil

Julia nodded her appreciation. After a fluke busy spell on Monday in the wake of the murder, Julia's café had returned to the ghost town it had become since Happy Bean had opened. Only a few of her most loyal customers were still popping in daily, Roxy being one of them.

"You don't think it's something I'm doing, do you?" Julia asked. "Maybe I'm just not good enough."

"You're the best baker this village has," Roxy said as she darted in to peck Julia on the cheek. "Things will return to normal soon. The novelty will wear off and people will realise they miss your fresh cakes. You'll see. I need to get back to the school, but I'll see you tomorrow."

Julia hoped she was right. For the sake of her business and keeping a roof over hers and Jessie's heads, she prayed Roxy was right.

After grabbing four large bottles of milk and having a little chat with Shilpa, who was trying to tell Julia she thought Anthony poisoned himself out of guilt for what he had done to the village, Julia returned to her café. The hairs on the back of her neck immediately stood on end when she saw Jerrad sitting at the table nearest the counter, staring around her café with a look of contempt.

"I tried to get him out," Jessie said desperately. "He won't budge."

"Threatened to '*bash my head in*'," Jerrad said with a little chuckle, his fingers performing the air quotes sign, something he used to do all the time to mock Julia. She had forgotten how much it irritated her. "Where did you find this one, darlin'?"

"Jessie lives with me," Julia said proudly as she marched back to the counter with the milk bottles in her hands. "And I'm not your '*darlin*', okay?"

Julia performed the air quotes, which only roused a small smirk from Jerrad. His right brow, the only one he could arch, darted up his forehead, and Julia was sure it reached closer to his hairline than she remembered.

"You did always have a thing for the waifs and strays," he said as he picked dirt from under his nails. "Couldn't pass a homeless person without tossing a quid at them. I always told you, you'd be better off ignoring them, so they learn their lesson."

Julia clutched her hand around Jessie's, which was shaking violently with rage. She squeezed hard, letting her know he wasn't worth it. She was sure if Jerrad knew the truth about Jessie, and the months she had spent homeless and how many of her friends had been murdered on the streets, it wouldn't have

Espresso and Evil

made a difference. It probably would have launched him into one of his political rants, where he was the only person allowed a valid opinion. Julia kept her mouth firmly shut, which was something she had learned to do many years ago. This time, however, it was to spare Jessie.

"Why are you here, Jerrad?" Julia asked flatly while Jessie busied herself putting the milk in the fridge under the coffee machine.

"Oh, you know," he said, suddenly standing up and pacing back and forth. "Just to check out the competition."

"I meant why are you in Peridale?"

"The same reason you are," he said, as though it was obvious. "For a fresh start."

Julia's stomach churned painfully, just as it had when she had first seen him. Not because she was learning that he was sticking around, but because that's what she had suspected all along. It seemed like the sort of cruel twist of fate that she was due, considering what she had kept from Barker.

"You *hate* this village," she reminded him. "It's *my* home."

"It's not *so* bad," he said with a shrug as he ran his finger along the shelf containing Julia's Peridale themed trinkets. He rubbed his fingers together, pretending to see dust, but Julia knew Jessie had cleaned that shelf only an hour ago because she was so bored. "Once you get used to it, it's almost – *quaint*. I can see why you were so obsessed."

"How did you ever marry this guy?" Jessie whispered as she listened from under the counter, stocking the fridge with the milk cartons as slowly as humanly possible. "He's a total *pig*!"

"I see you're still doing your baking," he said, walking over to the cake stand to peer inside. "Perhaps you and I could do some business? Since I'm running the coffee shop, it would be nice to appeal to the locals a little more."

"And put me entirely out of business?" Julia replied, suppressing her laughter. "You're out of your mind if you think I'd *ever* trade with you."

"I'd pay you reasonably," he said smugly. "What's the going rate these days? I can never keep up with the minimum wage. Always going up, while the effort goes down. That's what's wrong with our country. People are paid far too much for the most basic jobs. It's holding us back from growing."

Julia sighed, glad that Jerrad had cut his speech short. It was nothing she hadn't heard before. She used to tune it out, and nod and hum her agreement every so often, throwing in *'yes, dear'*, and *'you're*

Espresso and Evil

right' so he didn't question her. She couldn't believe she had ever been that woman.

"This *isn't* you," Julia said, looking around her café. "Peridale *isn't* you. You're a Londoner."

"I'm very adaptable," he said, meeting her eyes, his dark pupils looking right through her. "As are you. Taking in a young girl, hooking up with the local detective inspector. People do like to talk in this village. I hear you've become the woman to come to in a sticky situation too. Solving murders? That's not the Julia I knew."

"You don't know me," she reminded him, her voice stronger than it had ever been talking to him. "You only knew what you wanted to know."

Jerrad rested a hand on the counter, his eyes meeting hers, his lids flickering for a moment. She didn't recognise the look in his eyes. It made her anxious. She darted her eyes down to the counter, catching a flash of silver on his left hand. He was still wearing their wedding ring. Julia instinctively touched her own ring finger, which had been absent of a ring from the moment he had packed her things in bin bags and left a note on the doorstep. She had never regretted the decision to toss the ring in the River Thames. She thought about how much money she could have sold the diamond-studded band for, and how it would help keep her café afloat while she thought of new ways to tempt the customers back in. Just like the bundle of red notes in her biscuit tin, it was tainted money she would rather do without.

"We're going to have to learn to live alongside each other," he said as he stuffed his hands into his trouser pockets, making Julia wonder if he knew she had noticed the ring on his finger. "I'm staying at the B&B with some bonkers psychic woman offering me card readings every morning at breakfast. It's temporary until I find somewhere more permanent."

"You really are staying here," she whispered, her voice dark and suddenly angry. "You twisted little piece of –"

"I've invested every penny I've got into this business," he jumped in, his voice suddenly lowering as he leaned across the counter. "Anthony fleeced me, and now this is my way to get that money back. I'm not missing that chance, darlin'. Not for you, or anyone else in this village. See you around."

Jerrad's leather shoes squeaked on the tiled floor, and he sauntered slowly out of her café, making sure to eye up every small detail with a curl in his lip.

"Not missing his chance, eh?" Jessie said, bouncing up from the floor and folding her arms

Espresso and Evil

against her apron as they watched him walk across the village green. "Sounds like a motive for murder if ever I've heard one."

"It really does," Julia said. "For the man I remembered, the kind of money it takes to invest in a business like that is pocket change. If he's sunk all of his money into that coffee shop, he must not have had a lot to throw away in the first place. Did he seem a little desperate to you?"

"Reeked of the stuff," Jessie said, wriggling her nostrils. "And an aftershave that stinks of old men. Gross."

Julia sniffed up, his scent still lingering. Even after twelve years, the spicy fragrance that reminded her of the kind of detergent they used in hospital bathrooms still had the ability to churn her stomach.

"He's up to something," Julia whispered to herself as he walked back into his coffee shop. "And I'm going to find out what."

***

AFTER CLOSING THE CAFÉ, JULIA DROVE to the hospital where Sue worked. She sat in her car, as instructed during their call the day before, until her sister came out of the front doors. Sue wafted the clouds of smoke from the smokers as she hurried through, jumping straight into Julia's distinctive aqua blue Ford Anglia.

"She's here," Sue said as she pulled her phone out of her pocket. "It was hard to snap a picture of her, but I managed to get one when she was getting a coffee at the vending machine. My flash went off, but I blamed it on baby brain. She didn't ask questions."

Sue swiped through several blurry pictures of her feet and the hospital floor before landing on a perplexed looking woman who was staring straight at the camera while she slotted a coin into the coffee machine.

"That's her," Julia said. "She's the woman I saw laying flowers at the coffee shop after I was released from the station. What do you know about her?"

"Her name is Maggie Croft. She's forty-seven, and she's worked here for the past twenty-five years from what I can gather. She's nice enough, but a little quiet. She likes to keep to herself, but the walls talk. She left her husband six months ago, and they're already divorced. People have been saying she's been having an affair for years. I stayed out of it, but she's the first person I could think of when you called. I'm sure I even saw Anthony here a

Espresso and Evil

couple of times now that I think about it."

"Dad said Anthony was having an affair with a woman at the hospital back when they were still friends, and I saw her at the scene of his death, so there's no denying it."

"Do you think she *killed* him?" Sue asked. "She collects ceramic figures of pugs. I was her secret Santa three years ago. That's all I could get out of people. Bit weird, don't you think?"

"I don't think a person's tastes in ceramics makes them capable of murder," Julia said with a laugh. "But if she was having an affair with him, and she left her husband, my guess is she expected Anthony to leave his wife too."

"And when he didn't, she poisoned him?" Sue asked, her eyes widening. "That's the last time I accept a coffee from her on a night shift. How are things with you and Barker?"

Julia squirmed in her seat, wanting to talk about anything else but Barker.

"Not good," Julia said, her chest aching. "He can barely bring himself to look at me."

"I can get my Neil to talk to him," Sue offered, resting a hand on Julia's knee. "A man to man chat at The Plough over a pint? That usually does the trick."

"Thanks, but this is something I need to sort out myself," Julia said, smiling appreciatively at her sister. "Jerrad came into my café to gloat today. He's acting like he's sticking around to run the coffee shop."

"He's moving to the village?" Sue asked, twisting in her seat. "But he *can't*."

"He can, and he will. He said he sunk all of his money into the business and he's not going to see it wasted."

"Oh, Julia," Sue whispered, grabbing her hand and squeezing hard. "I'm so sorry."

Julia squeezed back. She was sorry too; sorry she hadn't dealt with Jerrad sooner. She had realised that if she hadn't prolonged signing the papers for so long, Jerrad might have signed his half and they would have been divorced. If she had told Barker that earlier in their relationship, it might have been easier to face Jerrad being in the village with the man she loved standing by her side to support her.

"Barker will come around," Sue said. "I promise. He loves you, and that's all that matters."

"And what about honesty?"

"You didn't *lie* to him," Sue said, chewing the inside of her lip. "You just didn't tell him the *truth*. There's a difference."

Espresso and Evil

"I don't think he sees it like that."

"Men usually don't," Sue said as she pocketed her phone and pulled on the door handle. "They see the world in shades of black and white and nothing in between. It's us girls who are cursed with that grey area. It makes us overthink, but it's also what makes us compassionate, caring creatures capable of brilliance. Barker sees that. He knows you, and he'll forgive you, given time. Men are like plants. You water and feed them, and the rest takes care of itself. The leaves may wilt, but a little tender love and care and they bounce right back. I need to get back. Debbie is covering for me. I said I was only nipping to the loo. I checked the schedule. Maggie finishes in ten minutes. She usually lingers outside for a cigarette before walking to the bus stop. You never heard any of this from me."

"Gotcha," Julia said, tapping the side of her nose. "Thank you."

"Don't ever forget that you're brilliant," Sue said into the car before closing the door. "My beautiful, brilliant, big sister. I'm going to go before I burst into tears. The lime is messing with my emotions today."

After a little pat on her bump and a final wave to Julia, she retreated back into the hospital, dramatically wafting her hands once again as she slipped through the cloud of smoke billowing from the patients.

Julia waited a couple of minutes before locking her car and walking towards the entrance. She checked her reflection in a car window, and dusted flour from her chocolatey curls.

She lingered back by the pay and display machine, smiling awkwardly at visitors as they glanced suspiciously at her while they tried to pay for their parking. After ten minutes, she began obsessively checking her watch, as more patients tossed their cigarettes to the ground and withdrew back to their wards, only to be replaced with more seconds later. She considered calling Sue to ask if she was sure she had the right time, until she saw Maggie slip out of the hospital.

Julia held back for a moment and observed the woman. Her eyes were stained red, her caramel blonde hair looked ratty and unwashed, and the duffel coat she was wearing over her blue uniform looked like it needed a trip to the dry cleaners. Compared to Rosemary, it was the difference between night and day. Julia watched as she fished her cigarettes out of her pocket, lighting one with shakier hands than some of the patients struggling to

Espresso and Evil

balance their crutches and their lighters. When her cigarette was lit, Julia took her moment.

Holding her breath through the smoke cloud, she looked ahead at Maggie, realising why she had recognised her as working at the hospital. She lifted her fingers up to the faint scar near her hairline where she had been struck by Charles Wellington's murderer in March. Maggie had been the nurse to remove the stitches. If it had been for the stitches alone, Julia might have forgotten her face entirely, but it was also the day she had signed and posted her divorce papers, so every detail of that day was engrained forever in her memory.

"*Maggie?*" Julia asked softly as she walked forward, her hands in her pockets. "Can I join you?"

Maggie scowled at Julia for a moment before a flash of recognition burned through her strained eyes. She pulled her cigarette out of her mouth and blew the stale smoke into Julia's face.

"*You!*" she sneered, venom in her voice. "What do *you* want?"

"I know what you've heard about me, but I can assure you, it's not true," Julia said, standing next to Maggie uninvited and leaning against the sign that told patients not to smoke at the entrance. "I didn't kill Anthony. I know you loved him."

"What do *you* know?" Maggie scoffed before sucking hard on her cigarette, tiny lines framing her lips. "How did you find me here?"

"I know you were in a relationship with Anthony Kennedy for many years before he died," Julia said, ignoring Maggie's second question. "I know you left your husband, probably in the hope that Anthony would do the same with his wife so you could be together."

The cigarette dropped from her lips and tumbled down her uniform. She stared at Julia for a moment before quickly dusting the grey ash off the blue fabric. She stamped on the cigarette and instantly pulled a fresh one from the packet. To Julia's surprise, she offered her one, which she politely declined. Roxy Carter's older sister, Rachel, had once persuaded Julia to try a cigarette when they were teenagers, but after one baby inhale she knew it hadn't been for her and one had never passed her lips since. Rachel was now in prison serving a life sentence for stabbing one of Julia's customers, but Julia didn't like to think the cigarettes were linked to the murderous streak, even as she was watching the woman at the top of her suspects' list light another cigarette.

"Anthony *loved* me," Maggie whispered through

Espresso and Evil

the side of her mouth as she struggled to light the tip with trembling fingers. "*Dammit!*"

She tossed the lighter to the ground, her hands disappearing up into her unkempt hair. She rested her head against the wall and clenched her eyes, the unlit cigarette falling from her lips as she began to cry.

"I don't think you were the only one," Julia said. "I don't know that for certain, but I've known Anthony for a long time."

"His wife *manipulated* him," Maggie said desperately, letting go of her hair and opening her eyes. "She *blackmailed* him to stay. He *couldn't* leave."

Julia thought back to the stylishly dressed woman who looked like she had had the weight of the world lifted off her shoulders in the wake of her husband's murder. It broke Julia's heart to think Maggie was another woman, just like her, who had allowed herself to be hoodwinked by a ruthless man.

"I think we both know Anthony wasn't going to leave his wife, and even if he did, he wouldn't have run into your arms."

"You don't know *anything!*" Maggie laughed coldly. "He used to laugh at you. The stupid little café girl with ideas above her station. He put you right in your place with his new business. He was going to bring me into it when it was doing better. He was going to open another location and let me run it. He loved me."

Julia knew it was no use trying to convince Maggie otherwise. Anthony might have been dead, but his ideas were well and truly alive in the poor woman's mind. Julia just prayed she would wake up and realise she was better than that before it broke her.

"I may just be a stupid little café girl, but I'm not going to sit back and take the blame for a murder I didn't commit," Julia whispered, leaning into Maggie so that nobody could hear her. "Where were you on the night Anthony was poisoned?"

Maggie stared at Julia for a moment as though she couldn't decide if she should take her seriously or not. A small laugh escaped her lips, but her nostrils flared, her expression flattening in an instant.

"I can't remember," she whispered, her bottom lip trembling. "Anthony had been ignoring my calls all week. He said he was busy, but I tried to go and see him that Saturday in the coffee shop. He told me to get out. I was upset, but I knew he'd come around. He always did, he just had a temper. I

Espresso and Evil

remember buying the bottle of vodka, but the next thing I remember is waking up in my flat the next morning. I didn't know he had died until I turned on the TV."

Julia hadn't been expecting such a frank confession, and from the horrified look that consumed Maggie's face, she hadn't expected to give it. Like all of the best secrets, it was almost impossible to keep them bottled up forever. Dirty laundry had a habit of floating to the top; Julia had learned that the hard way.

"Have you told the police any of this?" Julia asked.

"The police haven't spoken to me," Maggie said, stepping away from Julia. "If you tell anybody what I just told you, I'll say you're lying. Leave me alone."

Maggie pulled her cigarettes out of her pocket and headed towards the bus stop, asking every person she passed on the way for a lighter. Before she found one, a double decker bus eased into the stop, and she jumped on board. She sat by the window and glanced in Julia's direction before disappearing.

Julia hurried back to her car, the stench of cigarettes clinging to her pale pink peacoat, but her mind was whirring too quickly to care. She climbed into her Ford Anglia and set off back to Peridale, feeling like she had made a real breakthrough for the first time since Anthony had died.

CHAPTER 9

Sue reacted just as Julia expected she would when she sprung it on her that they were going to their father's for Sunday lunch, which is why Julia decided it was best to wait until late on Saturday night to tell her so she couldn't wriggle out of it, even if she tried her best to make every excuse in the world.

As they walked up the peaceful country lane to

Agatha Frost

Peridale Manor, Julia could sense the tension between them, which was manifesting in as many passive aggressive comments as Sue could muster.

"I suppose Katie hired caterers," Sue said, reaching to the low hanging tree above and tearing off a leaf. "I can't imagine that woman knows how to cook."

"You mean our *step-mother*?" Julia asked playfully, knowing how they both hated the term as much as each other. "After the last Sunday lunch, I'm surprised we're even being invited again."

"The one where Gran dumped the bowl of mashed potatoes over Katie's head when she dared to call Gran an '*old woman*'?" Sue replied as she twiddled the leaf between her fingers. "Ah, good memories."

"That explains why she wasn't invited today."

"It doesn't explain why *we've* been invited though," Sue said, tossing the leaf. "I hope Dad is okay. You don't think he's sick, do you?"

Julia felt like she had been hit with a brick. Her father had been acting nicer than usual, but she hadn't connected it to anything serious. Her mind flashed back to the day their mother had tried to explain her cancer diagnosis to them and how she wasn't going to be around forever. Anxiety knotted

Espresso and Evil

inside her.

"I'm sure he's fine," Julia said, gulping down the lump in her throat. "He looked fine when he came to my cottage."

"Did you check his temperature?" Sue asked jokingly. "If he had shown up unannounced at my house I would have demanded it. I'm sure the only time he's stepped foot in my cottage was on my wedding day. He said I looked '*nice*'. *Nice!* I was wearing a two thousand pound dress that I couldn't get out of to pee, and if I had fallen into a body of water, I would have drowned from the weight. I looked like a *movie star!*"

"At least you're modest."

"*Nice*," Sue echoed. "*Huh.* I bet nobody called Princess Di's dress just '*nice*'."

The conversation died down when Peridale Manor came into view. Like Oakwood Nursing Home, it was a grand and looming building that stood like a Goliath in the middle of the countryside. Julia had always thought the building had far too many windows to feel comfortable with.

"Ready?" Sue inhaled, her hand resting on her bump through her baggy shirt.

"I don't know."

"Well, it's too late for that," Sue strode up to the

doorbell and pressed it three times before stepping back. "It's now or never."

As expected, it wasn't their father or Katie who answered the door, but their elderly housekeeper, Hilary Boyle. She poked her head out of the door, her black liner-circled eyes bulging out at them as she polished a silver candlestick with a yellow rag.

"*You're late*," she barked, before swinging the door open and shuffling into the depths of the house.

"I wonder if they just keep her around because she's ingrained into the place?" Sue whispered as they closed the door behind them and shuffled into the giant manor.

A sweeping marble staircase spread up to the landing, providing all of the drama it was probably intended to. Julia couldn't imagine living in such a huge house, especially when there were only three of them. She wondered if they could go days without ever needing to see or speak to each other.

"*Girls!*" their father said, appearing from his study, dressed in a full tuxedo. "You made it."

Julia and Sue both looked down at their simple clothes. Julia had opted for a modest pastel green summer dress. Sue wore fitted jeans and an oversized t-shirt, which almost hid her bump. Julia suddenly

Espresso and Evil

realised Sue probably hadn't told their father the news of her pregnancy.

"I didn't realise there was a dress code," Sue mumbled through a smile. "Julia *forgot* to mention it."

"You're fine as you are," he said awkwardly as he adjusted his cufflinks. "Why don't you come through to the sitting room while Katie finishes getting ready?"

They followed their father through the large house, glancing awkwardly at each other as they did. Julia could feel the nerves radiating off his body, and it was making her nervous in turn. She couldn't shake what Sue had said about him being sick. She wasn't sure a tuxedo was the appropriate attire to break bad news to someone, but their father had never been one for convention.

"Wine?" he asked, already uncorking a bottle.

"I'm driving," Julia said, hoping the little white lie passed and that her father hadn't noticed that her car wasn't outside. "And Sue is doing this thing for work, aren't you Sue? What's it called? *Dry July?*"

"*Yeah,*" Sue mumbled, frowning at Julia as she nodded, the cogs in her brain clearly working overtime. "We're not drinking alcohol for charity."

"I thought you did that in January?" he asked,

Agatha Frost

pouring himself a glass.

"It was so successful, we're doing it again!" Sue exclaimed, clapped her hands together. "Cheers to that!"

Brian lifted his glass and tipped it to them before taking a sip as he stared curiously at his daughters.

"*Dry July?*" Sue whispered when their dad walked over to the drinks cabinet to put the red wine back.

"It was the best thing I could think of!" Julia replied quietly. "I was *trying* to help. Maybe today is a good time to tell him that's he's going to be a grandfather."

Sue pursed her lips, her cheeks burning even brighter. When their father returned, they both plastered artificial smiles on their faces as he handed them glasses of orange juice. Moments later, Hilary shuffled into the room and loudly cleared her throat. Their father nodded, and followed Hilary out of the room, motioning for them to follow him.

"He's acting stranger than usual," Sue whispered into her ear as they followed him into the dining room. "Are you sure you don't know what's going on?"

"You know as much as I do."

"It feels like a trap."

Espresso and Evil

Katie was already waiting for them in the dining room. She was sitting at the head of the long table, wearing a strapless white dress, which was cut low over her ample cleavage. Her face was plastered in makeup, and her plump lips were smothered in so much nude gloss, they were reflecting every light in the room. Her peroxide blonde hair, which looked like it had been encased in rollers all day, bounced out of her scalp at an angle that didn't look like it had grown out of her head.

"*Girls!*" she squeaked, clapping her hands together. "*Welcome!* Please, sit."

There were only four places set on the impossibly stretched out table. One at either end for Katie and their father, and two in the middle for Julia and Sue. Julia walked around the table, taking the one in front of the fireplace so she could keep her eye on the door in case they were planning any surprises.

Once they were all seated, they sat in stifling silence. Katie beamed out like a Cheshire cat, glancing from Julia to Sue as though it was their place to make conversation. Their father cleared his throat as he spread a napkin on his knee.

"No Vincent today?" Sue asked as she circled her finger around the lip of her orange juice.

Agatha Frost

"He wasn't feeling up to it," Katie replied quickly. "He's not himself at the moment."

Silence fell again until Hilary pushed in a trolley containing four bowls of tomato soup. Julia was glad of the distraction, even if it would only last until the bread rolls had run out.

"Delicious," Julia said. "Did you make it, Katie?"

Sue looked up from her bowl, pausing with the spoon next to her lips to send Julia a little grin. They both looked up at Katie, who appeared to be blushing under her caked-on makeup.

"Cooking isn't my strong point," she said with a shrug, her high-pitched voice reminding Julia of a little girl. "My talents lie in other areas, don't they, Brian?"

Sue choked on her soup, spluttering the red liquid all down her black t-shirt and onto the tablecloth.

"Katie is a great business woman," Brian said, smiling across the table at his wife, either ignoring or not noticing his daughter's reactions. "Tell them about your new venture."

"*Fake tan!*" Katie exclaimed, holding out her arms for them to see her luminous glow. "After the spa idea failed to get off the ground, I decided to go

Espresso and Evil

into product development. We're currently working on our first batch of '*Glow Like Katie*', but it should be hitting shelves soon!"

"Fake tan?" Sue asked, arching a brow. "Is that why we're here? For a sales pitch?"

"Well, no," Katie mumbled, looking a little hurt. "But it's something that is important to me. You could sell it in your café, Julia, and get the whole village glowing like Katie!"

Julia smiled politely, but she knew she wasn't going to let a bottle of the stuff pass her threshold. Just from the way Katie said it made it sound like Julia should be grateful for the proposal.

Instead of being a conversation starter, silence fell as they finished their soup. Sue appeared to have mentally checked out. She had started tearing her napkin into tiny pieces, something she did when she was anxious. Julia kicked her under the table and nodded, letting her know it was her time to speak. Sue mouthed '*ouch!*' and shook her head, so Julia kicked her again, but in the other shin this time. Sue jumped, her knees hitting the table, causing the cutlery to jump. Brian and Katie both turned to look at her.

"I *guess* I have something to share," Sue mumbled, looking under her brows angrily at Julia.

Agatha Frost

"I'm –"

"*Roast dinner!*" Katie exclaimed as Hilary pushed into the room with another trolley full of food.

She displayed the giant chicken in the middle of the table, and surrounded it with roast potatoes, honey-roasted parsnips, mash, boiled cabbage, stuffing balls, sweetcorn, and a giant vat of gravy. By the time they had finished passing the various items around the table and were tucking in, the food had almost turned cold.

"What did you want to say?" Katie asked as she slowly lifted a piece of chicken to her glossy lips.

"*Oh,*" Sue mumbled, blushing and stuffing her mouth full of cabbage. "*I'humpfergant.*"

"*Huh?*" Brian asked, tensing his brows and pointing his ear to Sue. "I didn't catch that."

Sue held her finger up, bobbing her head as she finished chewing. She looked at Julia, and rolled her eyes as she swallowed.

"I said I'm –"

"*Pregnant,*" Katie blurted out.

"*What?*" Julia mumbled, choking on a piece of chicken as she turned lightning fast in her seat.

"That's *my* line," Sue cried, looking from their father to Katie, bewilderment deep in her face. "*I'm* pregnant."

Espresso and Evil

"*We know*," Katie and Brian said in unison.

"How?" Sue asked, dropping her knife and fork and sitting back in her chair.

"We saw you at the maternity ward last month," Katie said, her hand reaching down to touch her white dress under the table, a distinct bump suddenly appearing before Julia's eyes. "I'm pregnant too."

Sue's nostrils flared, as anger clearly washed over her. Julia was too stunned to know what to say to calm her sister. The last time they had been invited to the manor house was with the rest of the village for a mystery announcement. Julia had expected Katie to announce she was pregnant then, not that she was attempting to turn the manor into a spa. That plan had been put to bed after her brother objected to the plans and was murdered. The thought of them having a baby hadn't crossed her mind since.

"I'm five months," Katie said, an excited squeak escaping her mouth as she stood up. "We're so happy, aren't we, Brian?"

Brian peered over his wine glass at his daughters, looking anything but happy. He seemed more concerned by their reactions than anything. His sudden reappearance in Julia's life, along with his unexpected compassion suddenly made sense.

"It's a little boy," he said, a smile breaking through his concern. "You're going to have a little brother!"

Sue's lips trembled as she attempted to speak, but the shock had silenced her.

"Congratulations," Julia said flatly, unsure of how she felt.

"*Yeah*," Sue mumbled, her eyes vacant as she stared at the butchered chicken carcass. "My brother is going to be two months older than my son."

"He'll *technically* be his uncle," Katie announced proudly as she cradled the bump, which was double the size of Sue's lime, with both hands. "Aren't you excited?"

Julia trained her gaze on Sue, willing her to make eye contact. Instead of saying anything, Sue screwed up her napkin, pushed out her chair and stormed out of the dining room. Brian jumped up, but Julia shook her head.

"Leave her," Julia said. "She's just in shock. We both are."

"A baby is an *amazing* thing," Katie said, apparently confused by Sue's reaction. "It will bring everyone together."

Julia stared at the bump, trying to imagine the

Espresso and Evil

fact she was suddenly about to have a baby brother who would be almost forty years younger than her. It only reminded her that she hadn't fulfilled her own dream of having kids. She tossed back the rest of the orange juice, wishing she had asked for wine after all.

When Julia didn't attempt to reassure Katie, she too stormed out of the room, leaving Julia and her father alone in silence. Hilary popped her head in, but quickly backed out when she caught Brian's firm gaze.

"Why does Sue *always* have to act like that?" Brian asked, the anger clear in his voice.

"Do you *really* need to ask that?" Julia asked, taking her turn to stand up and screw up her napkin. "You weren't there for us growing up, and now you're having another baby at the same time as you're about to become a grandfather. Are you honestly *that* blind?"

He gritted his jaw and flared his nostrils. He looked like he was going to try and defend himself, but he opted to drink the rest of his wine. Julia sighed and shook her head as she headed for the door.

"*Julia!*" he called after her. "Wait."

She almost didn't stop, but that little girl

waiting at the window for her father was still buried deep inside. She stopped in the doorway and turned back to face him as he slowly stood up.

"I'm sorry," he said, holding out his hands. "I own up to everything. I know I haven't been the best dad, but I'm not about to let that happen again."

"Good," Julia said with a firm nod. "Because he deserves better. But it doesn't change the past."

"We can change the future," he said. "It's not too late for any of us."

Julia nodded and half-smiled, wanting so desperately to believe that. She tried to imagine Sue seeing it the same way, but she would be surprised if Sue ever spoke to either of them ever again.

"I'm happy for you, Dad," Julia said, bowing her head. "I do mean that."

Julia walked out of the dining room and towards the open front door, where she could see Sue sobbing on the doorstep. She hurried along the marble tiles, her tiny heels echoing around the cavernous hall.

"Julia," her father called again. "I should have told you this before, but I've had a tip-off from a friend about Timothy Edwards. I think you'll want to speak to him. He lives in a small flat above Pretty Petals on Mulberry Lane."

Espresso and Evil

Julia didn't turn around. She almost couldn't believe her father was taking the moment to give her information on the case, even if she did make a mental note to remember exactly what he had said.

After closing the door, she slowly approached Sue, not wanting to startle her. She crouched down, wrapping her arm around her shoulders.

"That was supposed to be *my* news," Sue cried as she smudged her mascara streaks across her cheek. "She couldn't *wait* to jump in and ruin it. She ruins *everything*."

"It's just your hormones," Julia said, hugging her close to her chest. "It doesn't take anything away from your little lime."

Sue nodded through the last of her staggered tears. Julia unclipped her handbag and wiped away the mascara with her white handkerchief. When her face was clean, Julia hooked her thumb under Sue's chin and lifted her face up. They both smiled, and Julia knew they were both thinking the exact same thing: no matter what happened, they would always have each other.

"Let's get out of here," Julia whispered. "The Comfy Corner puts on a good carvery on Sundays."

Sue smiled through her sadness, the thought of food cheering her up. As they walked into the village, Julia stayed two steps behind, pulled her little recipe notebook out of her bag along with her small silver pen, and scribbled down '*Timothy Edwards – Pretty Petals*'. Out of all of the information she had learned at Sunday dinner, she knew that could prove to be the most useful.

CHAPTER 10

Still full from the carvery, Julia walked through the village to Mulberry Lane after walking Sue home. It was a lovely summer day with a clear blue sky above and a nice cool breeze bringing in the scent of freshly cut grass.

Mulberry Lane was the oldest known street in Peridale, with its mushed together cottages and shops, made from golden Cotswold stone, dating back to the 1700s. Its boutique shops were usually buzzing with life, but as Julia turned the corner onto the winding street, it was eerily quiet. At the end of the lane stood the antique barn, where she had spent a lot of her childhood with her father before her mother's death. If she had visited it since, she had no memory of it. She wondered what would happen to it now that Anthony was dead.

Keeping Anthony fresh in the forefront of her mind, she walked to Pretty Petals, the only florist in the village. After peering through the window at the beautiful display of coloured carnations in the window, she spotted a small, bright yellow door next to the shop. She pressed the buzzer on the intercom system and waited.

"*Hu-hello?*" a voice mumbled through the speaker system, barely audible. "*Who's there?*"

"I'm Brian South's daughter," Julia said, hoping that was enough. "My name is Julia. I wanted to ask you a few questions about Anthony Kennedy."

The intercom crackled again as though the man was pushing down on the button, but he didn't say a word. Julia wondered if she had just approached the whole thing entirely wrong, until the yellow door clicked and unlocked.

The stairway up to the small flat above the shop

Espresso and Evil

was dank and musty. It smelled like it was in a good need of an open window and a can of air freshener. Julia pushed on the door, hoping she would be able to breathe freely, but the theme continued throughout the flat.

Julia squinted into the dark. Despite it being the middle of the day, the curtains were tightly drawn, and there were no lights turned on. It took a moment for her eyes to adjust. When she saw the figure sitting in an armchair, she jumped back a little, her fingers clenching around her bag strap.

"Timothy Edwards?" Julia whispered, taking a deep step forward. "My name is Julia. Julia South."

The man reached out and clicked on a small lamp. Julia almost gasped but stopped herself. The man didn't look well at all. He was pale, and sweaty, with purple circles suffocating his eyes, which were straining from the light. He went to speak, but he erupted into a coughing fit. Julia hurried forward, placing her hand on the man's back, but he batted her away.

"I'm *fine*," he insisted through his suddenly mauve face as he fought back another attack of coughing. "I'm *f–f–*"

Julia hurried across the tiny flat to the kitchenette lining the back wall. The counters were covered in Chinese takeaway containers and unwashed plates. The low hum of buzzing flies filled her ears, making her shudder. She opened the cupboard above the kettle, relieved to see a clean cup. She filled it with water from the tap and returned.

Timothy sipped the water and it appeared to ease him a little. He sat back in his chair and rested his thinning hair on the headrest. He looked completely exhausted from the fit of coughing. Julia perched on the edge of the cluttered sofa next to him. On closer inspection, he didn't appear as old as she had first thought. He was in his late forties at the most.

"I'm Julia South," she repeated.

"I *know* who *you* are," he snapped as he slowly opened his eyes. "What do you want? I'm not well."

"I can see that," Julia said, edging forward and resting her hands on her knees. "I wouldn't have bothered you if I would have known, but I need to ask you some questions about Anthony Kennedy."

"What about him?" Timothy said with a small cough. "He's dead."

"I know. Somebody is trying to frame me, rather unsuccessfully, I might add, but I'd like to clear my name before the gossips keep running with the

Espresso and Evil

story."

"*Poisoned*," he said, which he followed with another bout of coughing. "Doesn't surprise me."

He attempted to laugh, but it was replaced with more coughing. He suddenly sat up, and the smell that wafted Julia's way made her wonder when he had last showered. It reminded her strangely of garlic.

"My father told me you and Anthony weren't on good terms."

"I wasn't always living here, you know," he said, staring down at the floor. "I'm *embarrassed*. I had a nice cottage and a family until Anthony came along."

"What did he do to you?"

Timothy met her eyes with a venomous gaze. She gulped, trying not to let the fear register on her face. She looked back to the door to the staircase leading back to the bright safety of Mulberry Lane, glad she had left it slightly open for an easy escape if needed.

"He *conned* me," Timothy said. "What else? That's what he did. I thought I was different, but I should have known."

"Conned you how?"

"Nothing that man said was true," he continued,

his eyes glazing over as he stared at the large stack of copies of *The Peridale Post* on the table, the latest sporting the headline '*COFFEE SHOP OWNER POISONED*'. "He had this way about him. He sucked you in and made you believe whatever he wanted. He could sell ice to the Eskimos. Rinsed me for all I was worth. I inherited valuable antiques from my mother. He told me they weren't worth the scrap money, but he offered me what he called a *good* deal. *Ha*! The man didn't know the meaning of the word. I trusted him, and then I lost everything. I lost my job, my wife, my kids, and for what? He's not even here now. To top it off, he came back for the painting because he knew I was a desperate man. He knew I would accept pennies for it."

"What painting?" Julia asked.

Timothy started coughing again, but this time it didn't subside. He stood up, instantly clutching his head. He swayed on the spot for a second before opening his eyes and stumbling across his flat and into the bathroom. Julia flicked on a second lamp, relieved at a little more light. It only showed how truly filthy the place was. She stood up and looked down at the couch, which was covered in a variety of different stains and smelled like it had spent a year or two in a swamp. She picked up the top

Espresso and Evil

newspaper, ignoring the article written by Johnny Watson, which also included details of her arrest and the ill-fated protest meeting. She put it down on the couch and sat, tucking her dress underneath her. She glanced at the bathroom as the sound of a flushing toilet echoed through the flat. Turning back, Julia's eyes landed on something that was sitting on top of the stack of newspapers that had been hiding under the most recent edition. It was a photo frame. She reached out and picked it up, glancing back at the bathroom as she did. The picture that looked up at her shocked her so much that her hand drifted up to her mouth.

Anthony Kennedy stared back at her with his glowing tan, yellow hair, open shirt, and pearly white teeth, with his arm around who appeared to be a much healthier, more youthful looking Timothy. Their heads were touching as Timothy reached out to take the photograph. She recognised Blackpool's south pier in the background.

The bathroom door opened and Julia quickly attempted to place the photograph back where she had found it, but it was too late. Timothy hobbled over and snatched the frame from her hands, his eyes wide with rage.

"What do you think you're doing?" he growled,

clutching the frame close to his chest. "How *dare* you come into my flat and touch my things."

"I didn't mean to," Julia mumbled. "I'm sorry. I should go."

She stood up, but the sick man loomed over her, his face nothing more than a shadow with eyes. Her heart thumped in her chest as she tried to remember where the door was.

"You were more than just friends, weren't you?" Julia asked, remembering what her father had told her. "You and Anthony were close in *another* way."

The flicker of his lids confirmed all Julia needed to know. She knew the look all too well and had felt it her fair share of times over the last week; it was heartbreak.

"He *used* me," Timothy croaked as he looked down at the picture. "He sensed my weakness. He used it against me, all to get to my antiques."

"That's awful," Julia whispered, reaching out and resting her hand on his, the fear subsiding. "I'm so sorry he treated you like that."

Timothy looked as though he was going to smile, but he coughed again. Julia decided she wasn't going to ask where he had been on the night Anthony was murdered. She didn't want to add insult to injury.

Espresso and Evil

"You mentioned something about a painting?" Julia urged, nodding her head in hopes of encouraging him.

"It doesn't matter now," Timothy said, tossing the frame to the ground before collapsing into the chair. "It's too late."

Julia looked down at the frame. The glass had cracked right down the middle, separating the two. Just looking at Anthony's face made Julia's blood boil. She knew he was cold, but she didn't think even he would prey on somebody's emotions for his own financial gain.

"I should go," Julia said, realising she wasn't going to get anywhere with more questioning. "Are you sure you're going to be okay?"

"It's just a cold," he said before coughing again. "I can't get the taste of metal out of my mouth. Don't mind if I don't show you out."

Julia stepped over the broken frame and towards the door. She turned back at the same moment Timothy flicked off the lamps, sending himself into darkness once more. She didn't know the man, but it broke her heart to leave another human being in such a state. This was something not even one of her cakes could fix.

Julia pulled her notepad and pen out of her

handbag as she made her way down the stairs. When she opened the door, she was glad to inhale the fresh country air again. It took her eyes a second to adjust, but the moment they did, she was scribbling down every detail Timothy had told her.

"*Julia?*" a familiar voice called out.

When she saw Barker walking down the street towards her, her heart skipped a beat. She smiled, never gladder than she was right then to hear Barker say her name. All she wanted to do was run into his arms, but she restrained herself.

"What are you doing here?" she asked, pocketing the notepad.

"I could ask you the same question," he said as he looked sternly down at her bag as she clipped it shut. "Somebody called about a hanging flower basket that's been stolen, so I thought I'd check it out."

"A hanging basket?"

"Sentimental value," Barker said quickly with a shrug. "Or so they say. I'm glad I've bumped into you. There was something I wanted to tell you."

"*Oh?*" Julia replied quickly, barely able to contain her smile.

"It's about the case."

"Oh," she said, the smile vanishing. "Here to

Espresso and Evil

arrest me?"

"The opposite, actually," Barker said as he stuffed his hands into his trouser pockets and rocked back on his heels. "You've officially been dropped as a suspect. You'll probably get a call tomorrow to confirm, so just act surprised."

"Why?" Julia asked, crossing her arms. "Has somebody been arrested?"

"I'm not at liberty to say."

"It's not your case."

"It's still an active case, though," he said, holding back the usual grin he gave her whenever she questioned his authority. "Since an arrest would be public record, I can tell you that you won't find anything if you go looking."

"Why have they dropped me?" she asked again, curious to know what vital piece of information had ruled her out of the running.

"I shouldn't be telling you this," he said, glancing over his shoulder to make sure they were alone. "The toxicology report came back. It showed that the arsenic that killed Anthony had built up in his system over a long period of time. The theory is that he was given small doses, little and often. Not enough to kill him in one go, but enough to be eventually fatal. It just so happened that his body gave in on that night, and whoever had been doing the poisoning had been keeping a watchful eye on him."

"And they tried to pin it on me because of the rivalry," Julia said. "Quite clever."

"My guess is whoever killed Anthony started doing it long before he found a fingernail in one of your cakes," he said reassuringly. "You were just in the wrong place at the wrong time."

"What are the symptoms of arsenic poisoning?" Julia asked.

"You don't think you've been poisoned, do you?"

"I feel fine."

"Good," Barker said, a genuine smile warming his lips. "I worried you might have been targeted as collateral damage. The symptoms are wide and varied, depending on how long the poisoning has been going on. It can remain undetected at first, but when somebody is succumbing to the toxin, they'll start sweating out of control, get stomach cramps, headaches, dizziness, vomiting, excess saliva, and a weird metallic taste in their mouth. The most peculiar one is that they might smell of garlic, which I almost couldn't believe when I heard."

Barker chuckled, but Julia wasn't laughing. She

Espresso and Evil

mouthed the word '*garlic*' to herself as she turned back to Timothy's door. Her heart stopped in her chest as she thought about the man she had just left alone in his dark flat. Julia hurried over to the door and pressed the buzzer over and over. When he didn't answer, she banged hard with her fists.

"We need to get in," Julia said. "I was visiting Timothy to ask about Anthony. They were having a love affair, which resulted in Anthony conning the man out of his valuables."

"So?" Barker asked, his brows creased low over his eyes.

"He had *those* symptoms!" she cried, her fists beating on the wood. "He said he had the taste of metal in his mouth! He thinks he has a cold, but he looked like he was on death's door."

Barker's eyes suddenly widened and he pushed Julia to the side. Before she knew what was happening, Barker's body collided with the door and it burst open with one swift bang. Julia scrambled after Barker as he ran up the stairs. He opened the door to the dark flat and felt on the wall for the light switch. By the time he had flicked on the light, Julia was right behind him.

"Don't look," Barker said, holding out his arm.

She stepped to the side, her mouth drying in an

instant. Timothy was slumped in his chair, the photograph from the frame resting on his chest. There was no doubt that the man was dead.

Without bothering about anything that had happened, she buried her face into Barker's chest.

CHAPTER 11

Julia barely slept a wink. She couldn't shake Timothy's pain from her thoughts, no matter how many times she tossed and turned. Just like Maggie, he had been deceived by Anthony's lies, but the bubble had burst for Timothy, which seemed to have taken a much worse effect on him than Maggie.

When she crawled out of bed on Monday morning ready to start another week at her café, her mind was filled with questions. Who had poisoned Timothy, and why? What did he know that could have led the police to the murderer if they had asked the right questions?

Julia skipped breakfast and sent Jessie to open up the café alone, deciding it was time she stopped avoiding her problems and talked to the one person who might actually be able to give her some answers to what was going on.

She burst through the doors of Happy Bean. There was already a line of people to the door, but that no longer surprised her. She made sure to look into the eyes of the people who used to be her customers as she passed them.

"*Hey*, there's a line – *Oh*, hello, Julia," Johnny Watson from *The Peridale Post* said, blushing as he adjusted his glasses. "I was just grabbing a coffee for research. It's for an article."

"Sure," Julia said, trying her best to smile, but not really caring any more about the reasoning behind the mass abandonment of her café. Ignoring the disgruntled people she had just pushed in front of, Julia turned to the frazzled barista, who didn't look like she had a clue how to cope with such a huge line.

"Where's Jerrad?" Julia demanded, glancing

Espresso and Evil

down at the floor where Anthony had died. "I need to speak to him."

The girl didn't say a word. She squeaked and pointed a shaky finger to a door at the far side of the coffee shop. Julia ignored the '*STAFF ONLY*' sign and burst in.

"*Julia*," Jerrad said, looking around the young boy he was speaking to. "What a *pleasant* surprise."

The boy turned around. It was Gareth Kennedy. He smiled meekly at Julia, barely looking her in the eyes.

"You can pick up your uniform on Friday," Jerrad said as he scribbled something down in a book on his desk. "Tell your mum I'll call her tonight."

Gareth nodded and shuffled out of the office without saying a word. Julia waited until he had gone before slamming the door and standing in its way so neither of them could leave.

"He seems like a good kid," Julia said. "You better not be corrupting him."

"I'm merely giving the lad a job here," Jerrad said, barely looking up from whatever he was writing. "He's at college with that street urchin you've got in your café. He was doing some stupid catering course, but I set him straight. After

Rosemary quit, and rightly so, it was time to get some fresh blood in the place. A coffee shop this busy doesn't run itself. You should know that. Actually, never mind."

"His father died last week," Julia said, ignoring his bait.

"They were practically strangers," Jerrad scoffed, snapping the book shut. "The boy barely knew the man. Why are you bursting into my office on a Monday morning? Come to reconsider my offer of a job? I'm sure it won't take *too long* to train you up to Happy Bean's standards. Old dogs *can* be taught new tricks, despite what they say."

Julia's nostrils flared, her fists clenching by her side before she even realised it. She wondered if Jessie's theory about giving Jerrad a black eye would make her feel better. She relaxed her fists, deciding it was the wrong time to find out.

"I need to hear everything you know," Julia demanded. "Another man has been poisoned, and I know you're hiding something."

"I don't remember you ever being so '*bossy*', darlin'," he said, performing his finger air quotes once more. "Take a seat and relax."

"I won't relax!" Julia cried, slamming her hand on the desk and startling Jerrad back into his chair.

Espresso and Evil

"Two innocent men are dead, you idiot. I need to stop this before anybody else is killed!"

"Me-*ow*," Jerrad purred, his brows darting up and down. "Where was this woman when the spark left our marriage?"

Julia recoiled, disgusted with the man in front of her. She wondered if it was possible for a person to be that ignorant to somebody's flaws for twelve whole years, or if Jerrad had just gotten worse in the two they hadn't seen each other.

"I'm not playing games," Julia said firmly. "Tell me everything."

Jerrad stood up and grabbed his car keys from a rack above the computer. He walked to the back of the office, where a back door opened onto the alley behind the coffee shop. Julia realised this was the entrance Barker had theorised that the murderer had used to gain entry to the coffee shop.

"Not here," he said, holding the door open and nodding out into the alley. "Let me take you out for breakfast. I've found this place that looks like a dump, but the food is fairly decent. I think it's called The Comfy Corner. Dreadful name."

"You must be out of your mind."

"Do you want me to share information, or not?" he asked with a leer. "Come on."

Jerrad walked through the door and turned into the alley. Julia looked back at the coffee shop, wondering how desperately she wanted to crack the case. If it hadn't been for seeing Timothy clinging onto the photograph of a man he had loved and been cheated by, Julia might have retreated to the safety of her dying café.

She didn't want to believe she would follow him, but that's just what she did.

***

THE COMFY CORNER WAS THE ONLY place in Peridale that could call itself a real restaurant. It was tucked away on a small backstreet directly across from the tiny library where Sue's husband, Neil, worked. From the outside, the restaurant wasn't much to look at, but everybody in the village knew it had the best food in Peridale, if not the whole of the Cotswolds.

Julia climbed out of Jerrad's sports car, glad to be in the fresh air again. The new car smell had practically knocked her sick when coupled with his erratic driving and overly spiced aftershave.

He held open the door of the restaurant, and she couldn't help but feel he was trying to take her out

Espresso and Evil

on a date, which was the last impression she wanted to give him.

The Comfy Corner was run by Mary and Todd Porter, two kind villagers in their sixties. When people talked about true love in the village, Mary and Todd were usually the standard that people looked up to. They had met when they were children at St. Peter's Primary School, and had been married since they were eighteen. Unlike Julia and Jerrad, Mary and Todd seemed just as in love as the day they had married.

"*Julia!*" Mary exclaimed. "Couldn't get enough of the carvery yesterday? Good to see you."

Mary's eyes landed on Jerrad and they bulged so hard out of her face, they practically popped out and rolled across the carpet. Julia wondered if Mary would wait until she had left to call everybody she knew to tell them Julia had been in there with a man that wasn't Barker. If gossiping were a sport, Mary would take the gold medal. She seemed to know everything before everyone, and it was known that you only said things in her presence that you were happy for the whole village to find out. Dot had suggested on more than one occasion that Mary had planted bugs around the quaint eatery, but Julia didn't quite believe that.

While Jerrad helped himself to three of everything from the breakfast buffet, Julia settled on a single slice of toast. She didn't want to give Jerrad the idea that she wanted to be there, even if her stomach did grumble as she walked past the bacon, sausages, beans, and scrambled eggs.

"Watching your figure?" he commented as they took a seat in the corner. "Probably for the best. You're creeping up to your forties."

Julia reminded herself why she was there and inhaled a deep, calming breath. She wished peppermint and liquorice tea were on the menu because she needed a cup to soothe her.

While Jerrad wolfed down his breakfast, Julia slowly buttered every millimetre of her toast, if only to figure out what she wanted to know first, and if he could be trusted.

"Where did you meet Anthony?" Julia asked, starting easy. "Sometime in the last two years I'm guessing?"

"Six months ago at a franchise convention in London," Jerrad mumbled through a mouthful of beans. "We bumped into each other by accident. He dropped all of his paperwork, and when I saw that he wanted to open a Happy Bean in Peridale, I knew I couldn't pass it up."

Espresso and Evil

"You said you sunk all of your money into the project," Julia said, trying to remember everything Jerrad had already told her. "How much?"

"Everything I had," he said, pausing for air before tucking into the next sausage. "It wasn't cheap keeping up with the younger women. Hair transplant, new teeth, abdominal sculpting. It all cost money."

"I *knew* you looked different!" Julia exclaimed, snapping her fingers together as she peered at his lower and thicker hairline.

"If I would have known the upkeep, I might not have switched."

Julia knew by '*switched*' he meant from her, a normal thirty-something with a normal body, to a young, blonde, skinny twenty-something. It had been a long time since Julia had realised that Jerrad had done her the biggest favour of her life. Deciding not to mention this, she thought about the next question.

"What did Anthony promise you in return for your investment?"

"That we would take over the world," Jerrad said sternly. "I should have known it was too good to be true. He told me we would have a location open in every town in England before Christmas, if only I –"

"Put up the money?"

"*Bingo*," Jerrad said. "He was good at the sale, I'll give him that."

"You're not the only person he conned," Julia said. "It was all he knew. Does the name Timothy Edwards mean anything to you?"

Jerrad paused, a slice of bacon hovering near his open mouth. He looked up at Julia for a second before cramming the meat into his mouth and chewing slowly. She took his silence as a yes.

"That's who died," she continued. "Did you know about his *real* relationship with Anthony?"

"I guessed something *funny* was going on," Jerrad said, as though he found the situation comical. "I heard a man's voice sometimes in the background of phone calls, and then when I came to the village, I realised it was him."

"You've met Timothy?"

"I went to his flat with Anthony about a month ago after one of our meetings," Jerrad said with a shrug. "Total cesspit. I don't know how a man could live like that."

Julia thought back to their apartment in London. It had been barren and devoid of any real personality, except for the calculated pieces Jerrad had approved. She wasn't surprised he had gotten on

Espresso and Evil

with Anthony so well.

"Did it have something to do with a painting?" Julia asked.

"So, you know about *the painting*," Jerrad said with a roll of his eyes. "Everybody wants to know about *the painting*."

"What do they want to know?"

"How they can get their grubby hands on it."

"Is it worth something?"

"Oh, like you wouldn't believe," Jerrad said, his eyes sparkling. "Anthony reckoned it could go for around a million."

"Certainly enough to murder somebody for," Julia said before taking a bite into her toast, which was now stone cold. She chewed it slowly and let her words stew in the silence. "Where is the painting?"

Jerrad crammed an almost full sausage into his mouth, his nostrils flaring angrily. From the way he looked glassy-eyed down at the plate, she knew his exact answer.

"You don't know," Julia said, sitting back in her chair with a small laugh. "*That's* why you're *here*. You want to get your hands on it."

"He wouldn't let me see it!" Jerrad snapped, leaning in across the table. "He made me wait outside the flat until he covered it up. I helped him carry it down, but he had chained sheets all around it. He only gave Timothy five hundred quid for it. He didn't know what it was worth. It's his own fault really."

"He *loved* Anthony," Julia snapped back, tilting across the table and meeting him halfway. "Anthony tricked him into falling in love with him for the sake of robbing him. It wasn't *his* fault. We all do stupid things in the name of love."

Jerrad narrowed his eyes before leaning back in his chair. He pushed his empty plate away, his right forefinger and thumb twirling the ring around on his left hand. Julia wondered if he even knew he was doing it.

"The slimy git could have hidden the painting anywhere," Jerrad said. "I wouldn't even know if I passed it in the street! I just know it's worth something, and he *owes* me that money! He turned me upside down and shook every last coin out of my pockets. I lost it all. That car outside is a rental. A *rental!* I'm disgusted with myself. He didn't put it in the business account like he promised. There's barely enough in there to keep that place afloat. We're running day to day."

"Not a nice feeling, is it?" Julia replied, thinking about the money in her biscuit tin once more.

Espresso and Evil

"Where does Rosemary come into this? I assume you're together?"

"*Casually* so," Jerrad said, his eyes tapering. "For now."

It took Julia a minute to realise what that meant, but a light bulb quickly sparked above her head, a crucial part of the puzzle slotting neatly into place.

"You're hoping she knows where the painting is!" Julia exclaimed, shaking her head as she held back the laughter. "Oh, Jerrad, you're no better than Anthony. You're using a widow for the sake of money."

"It's almost a million quid, darlin'," Jerrad remarked, his eyes widening with excitement. "It's only what I'm *owed*. She knows about the painting."

"But she doesn't know where it is either?" Julia asked. "Who else knows about the painting?"

Jerrad shifted uncomfortably in his seat. He glanced at the gold watch on his wrist, motioning for Mary to send the bill over.

"Gareth knows, doesn't he?" Julia responded for him. "That's why you've given him the job. You're hoping one of them is going to lead you to the pot of gold like a truffle pig."

"Kids soak up things," Jerrad mumbled as he pulled a twenty-pound note from his wallet and tucked it under his plate. "He *must* know something. They're bound to slip up eventually."

Julia couldn't believe what she was hearing. Dumping her things on the doorstep of the home they shared for twelve years was one thing, but using a boy and his mother to get to a dead man's treasure was a new low she wouldn't have thought even he was capable of.

"Why Peridale?" Julia asked. "And don't tell me you wanted a fresh start. If you invested with Anthony, you thought he was going to run the business and make you rich. You're not the type to get your hands dirty."

Jerrad stood up and fastened his suit jacket. He picked up a knife and held it up to his face. First, he checked his teeth in the reflection, which looked to have been replaced with a full set of veneers, and then his thick hair, which had been balding and receding the last time Julia had seen him.

"Why do you think?" he replied, a sudden softness taking over his voice before he turned and walked to the door.

Julia didn't move until she heard the roar of his sports car tearing down the road. She wondered what he had meant by that, but she didn't want to go there. The way he had touched his wedding ring

Espresso and Evil

had made her wonder if there was still a shred of the human being she had married in there somewhere.

"You've barely touched your toast, love," Mary said softly as she approached. "Would you like another go at the buffet? I won't charge extra."

"Thank you, but no thank you," Julia said as she stood up. "I have somebody I need to warn."

Julia headed straight for the exit and set off across Peridale, taking every shortcut she knew. She hurried down a small path and came out in front of Rosemary's cottage, her legs covered in nettle stings. She didn't care. She had already spent twelve years of her life making a mistake, she wasn't about to let Rosemary repeat that mistake. Jerrad might have shown an ounce of humanity beneath his ruthless exterior, but it wasn't enough. It only reminded Julia of how much she loved Barker, and how Rosemary deserved somebody like that, even if Barker could never bring himself to forgive her.

Julia unclipped the gate and hurried down the neat garden path towards the front door. Her finger lifted to the doorbell, but she stopped when she heard raised voices drifting through the slightly open sitting room window. She almost pressed the bell to make herself known, but she paused and decided to listen first.

"He's *gone*!" she heard Rosemary exclaim. "We can do what we want now. Be who we *want* to be. We don't even have to stay here."

"What if I *want* to?" she heard Gareth reply.

"Is it for that painting?"

"*No!*"

"Because if it is, we're never going to find it," Rosemary snapped, the freeness and contented calm gone from her voice. "Your father hid that thing good and proper, which means he died for nothing, but I *don't* care! We can start *fresh*! You and me, somewhere new. We can go to the coast! You always said you wanted to live by the sea."

"You're just as bad as him!" Gareth cried, his voice cracking at the top of his register. "All you care about is yourself!"

A door slammed, making Julia jump back. She thought about pressing the doorbell, but she had only come to warn Rosemary away from Jerrad. From the way she was talking, she wasn't the damsel in distress she had assumed she was.

Julia tiptoed down the garden path and back the way she had come, stinging her shins with the nettles once more. Wherever the painting was, Julia hoped it was beautiful enough to explain why it had driven everybody in Anthony's life to insanity.

CHAPTER 12

"All of this for a painting," Sue said as she sipped her raspberry lemonade at the table closest to Julia's counter later that afternoon. "I wonder what it looks like."

"It's probably some boring landscape," Jessie mumbled as she wiped down the tables for the fourth time since Julia had returned, despite there having been no customers. "Expensive art is always stupid. Galleries are pointless."

"It's a shame Rachel Carter is in prison for murder," Sue said with a heavy exhale as she remembered the owner of Peridale's only art gallery, which had remained closed since she had been locked up. "She would have been able to help."

"Are you forgetting the part where you destroyed her irreplaceable Georgia O'Keefe painting?" Julia reminded her with a playful smile.

"You asked me for a distraction!"

"And what about that priceless vase at Seirbigh Castle in Scotland?" Julia added, tapping her chin. "That was a family heirloom you sacrificed in another *distraction*."

"I'm clumsy," Sue said with a shrug as she rubbed her stomach. "What happened in Scotland stays in Scotland."

"What happened in Scotland?" Jessie asked, a confused expression on her face.

"*Nothing*," Julia and Sue replied in unison, having sworn not to mention the murder they had solved several weeks ago during a spa trip to Scotland, which their gran had won as part of a radio contest.

"Who are your suspects?" Sue asked, draining the last of her raspberry lemonade and shaking the

Espresso and Evil

cup for a refill. "You must have quite a few by now."

"I wish I did," Julia said with a sigh as she walked around the counter with the freshly pressed lemonade. "It seemed Anthony wasn't in short supply of people who wanted to kill him."

"It had to be somebody who knows about the painting," Jessie said. "So that could be practically anybody in the village the way people 'round here talk."

"We know Rosemary and Gareth know about it after what I heard this morning," Julia said, pulling out her notepad to read the things she had scribbled down. "And Jerrad, obviously. I don't know if Maggie knew about the painting."

"She could have still killed him though," Jessie suggested as she tossed the cloth down and took the seat across from Sue. "I saw people do the craziest things on the streets when they were drunk, especially on vodka. It always made them so angry."

"I totally forgot about that," Sue said, pulling her phone out of her pocket. "After you told me about Maggie's story, I remembered a text Debbie sent me. I never put two and two together until last night when I was in bed going through my messages. My storage was full, so I was deciding which ones to delete. *Ah*, here it is! '*You'll never guess who just turned up at my door drunk as a skunk*' with the crying laughing face emoji. That was at half ten on the Saturday night. I was asleep, but I woke up at four to throw up. Lime trouble." Sue paused to rub her stomach before continuing. "I sent her a message saying '*Omg! Who?*' with the confused face emoji at four minutes past four, and she replied '*Ceramic Pug Maggie! Came in and crashed out on my couch and then just jumped up and left ten minutes ago!*' with the shrugging girl emoji and the cocktail emoji, so I replied '*Omg! No way!*' with the shocked face emoji, and then *she* replied –"

"*Alright!*" Jessie cried. "*We get it!* I can't take anymore."

Sue pouted, locked her phone and tucked it away before crossing her arms and sulking.

"It rules her out," Sue said. "Anthony died before midnight, and she was at Debbie's between half ten at night and four in the morning."

"That's when he died, but that's not when he was murdered," Julia whispered, drumming her fingers on the counter as she hovered over Maggie's name with the pen. "Whoever poisoned him did it over a long period of time. She had access. It just means it wasn't her at the scene of the crime."

"What if Timothy poisoned Anthony and then

Espresso and Evil

poisoned himself?" Jessie suggested, her finger tapping thoughtfully on her chin. "Romeo and Juliet style, except everybody is dead when they say they are."

"You know Romeo and Juliet?" Sue asked suspiciously.

"Julia made me watch the film," Jessie replied, staring down her nose at Sue in a way only Jessie could. "The one with the dude from *Titanic*."

"That doesn't count!"

"It *totally* counts."

"It doesn't matter," Julia butted in before a full-scale fight broke out. "It's a good theory, brilliant in fact. It just doesn't feel right. I looked into his eyes, and I don't think he would try to frame me in the process."

"Who else knows about the painting?" Sue asked, staring off into the corner of the café.

"What painting?" a voice asked through the open door.

They all turned and watched as Brian ducked inside, a sheepish smile on his face. Sue looked like she was about to bolt and make for the door, so Julia hurried around and stood between them, smiling kindly at both of them.

"Thanks for coming, Dad," Julia said,

apologising with her eyes to her sister. "That is actually a question I was hoping you would be able to answer. Tea?"

"Yes, please."

Julia quickly made him a pot of tea. She put it on a tray with a cup, saucer, milk, and sugar, before remembering what he had told her about the sugar. She quickly removed it and carried it to the table, which he had taken directly next to Sue's. She was trying her best to look in every direction apart from his.

"So, you want my antique expertise?" he asked as he pulled off the teapot lid to check if the tea had steeped. "I can't say I've been asked for that in a while. What's this painting? Something you've found in your attic?"

"Not *exactly*," Julia said, pulling up the chair across from him and catching Sue's eye to let her know it was okay to speak. "We don't actually know what the painting is, or where it is."

"Is this connected to Anthony?" he asked as he poured himself a cup of tea.

"You know the painting?" Jessie asked.

"No, but everything seems to be connected to him at the moment, which is why I guessed you called me here."

Espresso and Evil

Julia smiled her apologies. She wondered if a small part of him had thought she had called him to talk about what had happened at Sunday dinner. That was currently the bottom of Julia's priorities list, even if she had noticed it was a good opportunity to get her sister and father in the same room again.

"What does it look like?" he asked. "Who painted it?"

Julia looked at Jessie, who looked at Sue, who stared down at her nails.

"I need a manicure," she whispered absently.

"We don't know," Julia said, pursing her lips at her baby sister. "We don't know anything other than that it could sell for nearly a million pounds, and it's worth slowly poisoning a man for."

"A *million*?" Brian replied, sucking the air through his teeth. "Not many paintings fetch that. It has to be something special by one of the greats. That narrows it down slightly."

"Do you think you would be able to make some calls?" Julia asked hopefully, nodding her head, feeling like she was clasping her fingers around one of the final puzzle pieces.

"It won't be *that* easy," he said after sipping his tea, ripping that puzzle piece away from her.

Agatha Frost

"Anthony didn't exactly work by the book. If he were buying a painting to sell it, he wouldn't have been going through the proper channels. Do you know who the previous owner was?"

"Remember how you gave me Timothy Edwards' name?" Julia asked, the name sticking in her throat. "He was poisoned yesterday. I'm certain it's connected to this painting."

"Edwards, you say?" he said, furrowing his brow and looking down at the teapot. "*Edwards. Edwards.* How do I know an Edwards? I got Timothy's name from an old friend, but now that I think about it, I know an Edwards of my own. I'm sure the name rings a bell."

Julia stared hopefully at him and waited for a grand revelation. After less than a minute of thinking, he shrugged and resumed his tea.

"Have you asked Rosemary if she knows anything?" he asked, setting his cup back onto the saucer. "From what I can remember she wasn't all that bad at antiques. She had style and taste, and that accounts for a lot. You can buy something worthless and give it worth by the way you position it or frame it. She used to help out in the shop with your mother when I lacked inspiration."

Sue suddenly sat up straight in her chair at the

Espresso and Evil

mention of their mother. She whipped her head to face him to let him know he shouldn't have dared to speak about their mother. Julia pleaded with Sue with her eyes to calm down, but it didn't seem to make any difference.

"I overheard Rosemary saying they would never find the painting," Julia said, hoping the detour would give Sue a moment to calm down.

"That doesn't mean she doesn't know *what* it looks like," he suggested as he filled his teacup again and added more milk. "Or at least *who* painted it."

Julia sat back in her chair, realising he was right. She stood up and hurried behind the counter to grab her car keys and coat.

"I won't be long," she said to Jessie. "Sue will stay and keep you company, won't you, Sue?"

Sue grumbled and nodded, not looking up or speaking as she obsessed over her nail beds once more.

"Dad?" Julia called as she opened the café door. "Are you coming?"

"Oh," he mumbled, draining the last of his tea before standing up. "Right. Am I coming with you?"

"You're the expert," Julia said.

"I suppose I am," he replied with a nod as he hurried after her. "See you later, girls."

They both grunted back, neither of them seeming able to communicate like proper human beings when the time called. Ignoring that, Julia unlocked her tiny car and she set off towards Rosemary's cottage for the second time that day.

***

WHEN THEY WERE OUTSIDE THE cottage, Julia was surprised to see a removal van parked outside, and she was even more surprised to see that they were taking things into the cottage, instead of out.

They jumped out of the car and followed the movers through the open front door. The men carried an ornate chair up the stairs, but Julia and her father slipped through to the bright, open-planned kitchen.

"Julia?" Rosemary exclaimed from the stove where she was stirring something in a pot. "I was just making lunch. Brian, is that you?"

Rosemary turned off the gas and squinted at Julia's father.

"It's me," he said. "Long time no see."

"What has it been?" she asked with a chuckle. "Twenty-five years? Or even longer? I haven't seen

Espresso and Evil

you since – *well* – you know."

Rosemary's eyes flickered sympathetically to Julia. She knew exactly what Rosemary was talking about, but she let it glide over her head because she had more pressing things to discuss.

"I'll make some tea," Rosemary mumbled as she shuffled over to the kettle to distract herself. "Still take two sugars, Brian?"

"Katie's got me on the no-sugar thing," he said, patting his small stomach. "Diabetes scare."

"Ah, yes," Rosemary said, grinning over her shoulder. "The *younger* model."

Unlike most people, Rosemary didn't look offended that Brian had married a woman almost twenty years younger than him. Instead, she almost looked proud. It took Julia a moment to realise there was probably a similar age gap between Rosemary and Jerrad. It sent a shudder down her spine. Not because of the difference in age, but because Rosemary seemed pleased with the man she had managed to catch. Julia wanted to tell her there and then that no matter how much younger Jerrad was, she deserved far better, especially being such a stylish and vivacious woman.

They took the tea through to the conservatory, and Julia stopped in her tracks when she saw Barb sat in one of the wicker bucket chairs, staring out at the garden while the young nurse from Oakwood painted her nails red. Unlike when she had seen her at the nursing home, her thin grey hair was out of its bun and flowing down her shoulders. It was so long it rested in her lap.

"Barb, you remember Brian and his daughter?" Rosemary asked jovially as she set a cup on the table next to her mother-in-law.

Barb looked Brian up and down, a strained smile twisting her lips. When she spotted Julia, she smiled a little easier, but there was still a flicker of confusion at their visit.

"Barb's moving in for a while," Rosemary said, the smile growing from ear to ear, her cheeks blushing a little. "Thinks I need the help."

"It's the least I can do," Barb said as she looked down at her freshly painted nails. "Yelena, will you be a dear and fetch my blood pressure pills from upstairs? I think I'm due a top up."

"Of course," Yelena said with a soft smile, her Eastern European accent sticking out. "One moment."

The tall and pretty young nurse excused herself from the room, smiling at Julia as she passed.

"Yelena was kind enough to leave Oakwood to

Espresso and Evil

be my private nurse," Barb explained when she met Julia's eyes after she had watched Yelena hurry down the hallway and up the stairs. "She's a lovely girl. You find the Ukrainians are very grateful for the jobs."

Julia was a little shocked when nobody picked up on her casual racism. If it had been her gran, she would have corrected her immediately, but she held her tongue because it wasn't her place.

Rosemary pulled two more chairs from the side of the room, and she took the one next to Barb where Yelena had been sitting. Julia and her father sat across from them, awkwardly sipping their tea as they sat in silence. She was almost glad when she heard Yelena padding down the carpeted stairs, if only for something to break the silence.

She returned with a packet of pills in her hand, from which she popped out two. She passed them to Barb, who slotted them between her lips with shaky hands. She sipped a little of her hot tea before tossing her head back. Without the safety of her chess-playing friends to surround her, she looked frailer and much older than Julia first remembered.

"I'm surprised you've left Oakwood," Julia said after sipping her tea. "You seemed to enjoy it there."

"They'll keep my room open," Barb replied with

a smile as she reached out and grabbed Rosemary's hand. "I might not have been close with my son, but Rosemary and Gareth are the only family I have left now."

Rosemary smiled sweetly while glancing down at Barb's bony fingers. Julia wasn't sure if she was imagining it, but Rosemary seemed to want to do nothing more than pull her hand away.

"There is a purpose to our visit," Julia said as she rested her cup on the window ledge. "We hope you could help us with some information regarding Anthony."

"*Information?*" Rosemary asked, a shaky smile covering her lips. "About what?"

"A painting," Brian jumped in. "A valuable painting that your husband bought and intended to sell for an incredible profit. Do you know anything about that?"

Barb didn't react, instead looking at Rosemary, whose lips were shaking out of control as she attempted to smile. She sipped her tea and swallowed hard before tilting her head and smiling a little firmer.

"I'm sorry, I don't know anything about a painting," Rosemary said, avoiding Julia's gaze and staring right at Brian. "I didn't get involved with

Espresso and Evil

Anthony's work."

Julia almost called her a liar right then, but she gritted her teeth and forced herself to keep quiet. If she revealed what she knew, it would out her eavesdropping earlier in the day.

Rosemary opened her mouth to say something, but the sound of smashing glass startled them all.

"What are they doing with my things?" Barb cried, jumping up and scurrying down the hallway with Yelena hot on her heels. "Not my glass vase! What am I paying you for?"

Rosemary continued to sip her tea, smiling as though nothing was wrong. Compared to the free smile Julia had seen the day after Anthony's death, this one was as fake as they came.

"Do you know Timothy Edwards?" Julia asked, her eyes trained on Rosemary's.

Her lips twitched, her smile freezing as she considered her response. She sipped her tea again, swallowing as though she was drinking a cup of sand.

"No," Rosemary said, her hand patting her chest as she forced it down. "Will you excuse me for a moment?"

Rosemary put her tea on the table next to Barb's and hurried out of the conservatory.

"She's lying," Julia whispered. "Why is she lying?"

"Maybe she's found the painting?" her father theorised.

"In a couple of hours?" Julia replied with a shake of her head. "No. She was talking about fleeing Peridale this morning, and now she's letting her mother-in-law move in. I don't understand."

"That's just the kind of woman Barb is. It's almost impossible to say no to her. I know she says she didn't like Anthony, but he didn't like her much either. He visited her out of guilt, even if he didn't really understand the concept of guilt."

Leaving her tea almost untouched, Julia stood up, deciding nothing Rosemary said could be trusted anymore. They slipped out of the cottage as two men heaved a chest of drawers up the stairs while Barb dictated from the top.

"If you hear anything about the painting, make sure to call me," Julia said as she dropped her father off outside Peridale Manor. "Tell Katie I said hello."

He assured her that he would, seeming touched by the gesture. Julia knew it was going to take more than a baby to build long since burned bridges, but it was a better place to try than any.

As she drove back to the café, she racked her

Espresso and Evil

brain to try and figure out the truth about what had happened on the night her café had been broken into. She felt like the answer was staring her straight in the face, but she was missing a vital piece of information that was wriggling right under her nose.

CHAPTER 13

When Julia returned to the café, Sue was standing behind the counter flicking through a gossip magazine. She let out a yawn before looking up and spotting Julia.

"Jessie's gone for a driving lesson with Barker," Sue said as she flicked through the magazine. "Do you think I'll suit this dress after I've pushed out the pumpkin?"

Espresso and Evil

Julia shrugged. She hung her jacket on the hook in the kitchen and tossed her car keys on the counter. She smiled to herself, glad that Barker wasn't taking his anger out on Jessie. She was an innocent party stuck in the middle of two people who didn't know what to say to each other to make everything right.

"He asked where you were," Sue said, slapping the magazine shut as she stretched out, letting out another yawn. "Told him you'd gone off somewhere with Dad. Wasn't sure if you wanted him to know you were snooping."

"I wasn't snooping," Julia said with a roll of her eyes. "I was just asking some questions."

"Same difference," Sue said with a chuckle. "He seemed pretty upset that you weren't here. I think he wanted to talk to you."

Julia thought back to the brief moment they had shared after finding Timothy's body. She had buried her head in his chest, and he had put his arm around her, holding her silently until the police arrived at the scene. As soon as the scene was secured, they parted ways, and she wasn't sure how they had left things. She hoped it would have brought them closer together again, but she also knew it was possible it was a momentary blip, and Barker might never want to touch her again.

"Are you just assuming he was upset or did he actually look upset?" Julia asked as she dropped a peppermint and liquorice teabag into a cup.

"He pulled this face." Sue scrunched up her face and pushed out her bottom lip. She looked like a Cabbage Patch Kid. "And then he started sobbing and fainted to the floor screaming '*Julia*'!"

Julia tossed a dry teabag at Sue. It hit her on the side of the face.

"I'm glad my life is so amusing to you."

"Oh, cheer up, big sis," Sue said, tossing the teabag back. "Okay, so I might have stretched the truth *a little*, but he did look disappointed. And he's spending his lunch break giving Jessie a driving lesson. That must mean something."

"Jessie hasn't done anything wrong."

"Neither have you," Sue said with a shrug. "Still being married to a pig isn't a crime. So what that you didn't tell him? I bet he hasn't told you every detail of his past."

Julia dropped her head guiltily as she poured hot water into the small cup. She thought back to the time Barker had shared his past with her, about how his fiancé had died. She had almost shared her own past with him after that revelation, but it felt cheap

Espresso and Evil

in comparison. He had told Julia she was the first woman he had loved since, which dug the guilty knife even deeper into her chest.

She pulled on the string of the teabag and bobbed it up and down in the water as she gazed out of her café window at the quiet village green. People seemed to be heading to Happy Bean's, avoiding looking in her café's direction. She wondered if it was time to accept her fate and start thinking about another route she could take, but it ached to think she wouldn't have her café to come to every day.

"Maybe I could do corporate events," Julia thought aloud before blowing on the hot surface of the water. "Or wedding cakes."

"*Boring*!" Sue exclaimed. "I went for my scan this morning. I was going to tell you before, but Dad came, and I didn't want to show –"

Screeching tyres interrupted Sue before she could finish her sentence. They both turned to the window in time to see Jessie drifting around the corner of the village green in Barker's car. Dot, who was tearing out the weeds that were poking through her garden wall, jumped back, tumbling over the low wall and into her garden. Julia caught a flash of Jessie's hand waving her apology before she sped off again, turning and speeding past St. Peter's Church like she was drag racing.

"For the sake of Peridale, I hope that girl *never* passes her test," Sue said with a nervous laugh. "She's *lethal*!"

"She's learning," Julia said, as hopefully as she could muster. "You failed your test three times, remember?"

"But I didn't kill anybody in the process!" Sue exclaimed as she grabbed her handbag from under the counter before pulling out a bottle of red nail polish. "I hit that cat, but it sprung right up and ran away with eight lives still intact. Barker is braver than me to get in a car with her. What do you think of this colour? Does it clash with the bump?"

Julia chuckled as she sipped her tea. She looked out of the window at the village green again, and something outside Happy Bean caught her attention. She craned her neck in time to see Jerrad bolting out of the coffee shop as the stressed young barista from earlier burst through a crowd of people, tossing her apron to the ground as tears streamed down her face. She ran across the road, narrowly missing the bonnet of Barker's car as Jessie made another erratic lap of the village green.

"Drama at Happy Bean," Julia whispered over the top of her tea. "Looks like she's just quit."

Espresso and Evil

"You could sound *a little* less happy about that," Sue replied with a wink. "Serves the man right."

Julia sipped her tea, letting the peppermint and liquorice warm her throat, the familiar sweetness perking her mood after the disjointed morning. She watched the girl sprint across the village green, mascara streaking her cheeks. Julia put down her tea, and walked around the counter.

"Stay here," Julia said. "I won't be long."

"*Again?*" Sue cried as the red-tipped brush touched her thumb nail. "Where are you going?"

"To gloat," Julia said with a shrug and a twinkle in her eye. "If you can't beat them, join them."

Leaving Sue in the café to paint her nails and attend the non-existent customers, Julia hurried across the village, waiting until Jessie had passed to cross the road. A little smile tickled her lips when she looked through Happy Bean's window and saw Jerrad behind the counter, attempting to work the complicated computer screen till while a line of frustrated people tapped their feet

"Having some staffing trouble?" Julia asked, trying her best to sound concerned.

"The little brat quit!" Jerrad cried, hovering over the screen, his eyes scanning the dozens of different options. "What did you say you wanted?"

Agatha Frost

"A caramel latte with an extra shot," Jeffrey Taylor, Billy's father, said. "Oh, hello, Julia. Is that your Jessie bombing around the village in that car? She's almost as bad a driver as my Billy. I've tried teaching him, but he's a lost cause."

"Let's hope they never get in a car together then," Julia said, trying to smile through her disappointment that Jeffrey hadn't come to her café for his usual order.

Jerrad peered under his brows, his eyes almost pleading with Julia to help. He somehow managed to put the order through the machine before taking Jeffrey's money with shaky hands. When he turned to the coffee machine, he wiped the visible beads of sweat from his forehead with one hand while the other rubbed the faint stubble on his jaw.

"*Erm*," he mumbled. "Coffee. *Right.*"

Julia exhaled heavily, not wanting to believe what she was about to do. She walked around the back of the machine and slipped behind the counter, pushing Jerrad out of the way.

"You like it quite strong, don't you Jeffrey?" Julia asked over her shoulder with a smile. "No custard slice today?"

"Watching the figure," he said with a pat on his completely flat stomach, which she knew was

Espresso and Evil

smothered in inky tattoos under the fabric.

Julia quickly made the order with ease. It was a little more complicated than the machine in her café, but it did the same thing. She had always wondered why steaming milk and filtering ground coffee needed so many buttons and knobs.

While Jerrad figured out the drinks orders on the till, Julia quickly produced them, switching with ease between coffee, cold drinks, and tea. She wasn't sure if she was working to Happy Bean's standards, but she knew she was working to her own, which had been good enough for the village until recently. When the last of the customers took their drinks, Jerrad turned to Julia with a relieved smile covering his sweaty face.

"We make quite the team," he said with a smirk. "You just saved my bacon."

"Don't get any funny ideas," Julia said, extending a finger in his face. "Even I couldn't watch you try to figure this out. I did it for the customers, *not* for you. They might have stopped caring about me, but that doesn't mean I've stopped caring about them."

Jerrad held his hands up, before clasping them together and bowing his head in thanks.

"I rather like this new, feistier Julia," he said,

taking a step forward. "You've changed."

"I've grown."

"We both have."

Julia held back the laugh. She looked at his fake hairline, fake teeth, and impossibly flat stomach, which used to poke out of his shirts.

"There's a difference between growth and change for the sake of change," Julia said with an arch of her brow. "I need to get back. I have an empty café to run."

Julia slipped around the side of the coffee machine and walked across the sterile coffee shop towards the door.

"*Wait!*" Jerrad called after her. "Let's talk."

"About what?"

"Us."

Julia didn't suppress the laughter this time as Jerrad walked around the counter after her.

"Unless you want to talk about us actually getting divorced, there is no '*us*'," Julia said, folding her arms across her chest.

Jerrad reached out and grabbed her hand, his cold wedding ring burning against her skin. She was so stunned, she didn't immediately pull away.

"Don't you feel it?" he asked, pulling her in slightly. "The spark?"

Espresso and Evil

"I think it's just indigestion, *darlin'*," Julia said, ripping her hand away as she stared into Jerrad's eyes, sure that he was just about to kiss her. "I think you need to read the instruction manual before your next wave of customers floods through the door."

Julia turned on her heels, pleased with her confidence. She had never had the guts to stand up to Jerrad, but looking into his eyes and saying exactly what she wanted felt refreshing. Barker had never tried to censor her, and she knew it had made her a better, stronger woman.

She pulled on the door and set off down the street, feeling Jerrad hot on her heels.

"*Julia!*" he cried after her. "You're *still* my wife."

"We're separated," she called over her shoulder. "It's just a piece of paper. It doesn't mean anything."

Knowing that Jerrad was going to chase her right back to her café, where she would be stuck in a room with him, she made a detour and cut across the village green, glancing in Sue's direction to make sure she wasn't being bombarded with customers; she wasn't, and she was still paying close attention to painting her nails.

"You *need* to listen to me," he cried, jogging to keep up as she hurried across the grass.

"I don't *need* to do anything."

To her surprise, Jerrad's fingers wrapped around her wrist, yanking her back. She stopped in her tracks, feeling a little pop in her shoulder. She tried to pull away, but his grip was firm.

"I said, you need to listen to me," he said, his voice darkening as he stared deep into her eyes. "You're my wife, and I made a mistake."

Julia stared down at the fingers tightening around her wrist, turning the skin there white, and her fingers bright red. She pulled again, but he was holding on tightly.

"Let *go* of me," she said, her free hand clenching. "Now."

"You're my wife!" he repeated, as though it meant something. "Twelve years, darlin'. It means something. You and me, the dream team."

"It was a nightmare," Julia said through gritted teeth as she continued to yank. "I said, let go –"

Screeching tyres interrupted her, making them both turn to face St. Peter's Church. Barker's car burst over the concrete lip of the village green, landing with a crash on the grass. Instead of stopping, the car sped up, racing towards them at lightning speed. Frozen to the spot with Jerrad still gripping her, Julia closed her eyes and waited.

There was another screeching, as tyres and grass

Espresso and Evil

collided. Julia peeked through her lids, and let out a huge sigh of relief when she saw the car had ground to a halt only steps away from them. Through the pounding of her heart, she let out a small nervous laugh.

The driver's door opened. What Julia saw was even more shocking than the car racing towards them. Jessie wasn't the one who had been driving, it had been Barker.

"Get off her," Barker snapped as he slammed the door before marching towards her.

To Julia's surprise, Jerrad did let go of her in an instant, but instead of stepping back and apologising, he walked towards Barker, meeting him halfway. Julia clutched her sore wrist, turning as Jessie jumped out of the passenger seat.

"Or *what*?" Jerrad sneered, laughing in Barker's face as their chests bumped together. "You gonna arrest me, PC Plod?"

Barker smiled down at Jerrad, who was several inches shorter than him. He blinked slowly, the smile growing, before turning into a sneer. Julia noticed Jerrad's fingers tucking into his palm. She stepped forward, unsure of what to do.

Before Barker could do anything, Jerrad reacted first, his fist striking Barker hard in the stomach. He doubled over and stumbled back before falling to the ground. Julia screamed out and ran to his side.

"You *idiot*!" she cried up at Jerrad, her hands clutching Barker's shoulders.

"She's *my* wife," Jerrad said, before spitting at Barker's feet on the grass. "Nobody is going to –"

Jerrad didn't get to finish his sentence. Jessie's fist struck his nose, and with a crack and a spurt of blood, he fell to the ground completely unconscious. Jessie doubled back, clutching her fist to her stomach as she winced in pain.

"*Ouch*!" Jessie mumbled through her red face. "I knew he was a bonehead."

Barker stumbled to his feet with Julia's help as he caught his breath. Julia looked around the village as people ran from every direction, including two police officers.

"If anybody asks, I punched him," Barker said, tapping Jessie on the shoulders. "Get out of here."

A car pulled up in front of Julia's café just as Sue ran to the door, her eyes wide. Their father climbed out of the car and looked down at Sue. Instead of explaining anything, she grabbed his hand and dragged him to the scene, with her other hand clutching her tiny bump.

"What did I miss?" Sue cried, her arm wrapping

Espresso and Evil

around Jessie's shoulders as she looked confused between them. "Jessie, are you okay?"

"I think I've broken my thumb," she muttered, looking down at her hand, which she was still clenching. "But it was worth it."

"You need to ice it," Julia's father said.

"There's ice at Happy Bean," Julia replied, glancing down at Jerrad as he started to come around with a groan. "He's not dead."

"Shame," Jessie mumbled as they walked towards the coffee shop. "I was hoping to hit him so hard he flew out of Peridale and landed on the moon."

Barker held back, pretending to clutch his hand as he began to explain what had happened to the two police officers, who Julia recognised as the ones who arrested her and Jessie. Barker caught her gaze, and they shared a smile. He winked at her, before reapplying his fake hurt expression. She had a feeling things were going to be okay after all.

Once they were in the empty coffee shop, Jessie and Sue sat in two of the pleather armchairs, while Julia hurried behind the counter and scooped a handful of ice into a tea towel, which she secured in place with an elastic band from a bag of chocolate flakes. Julia's father hovered back, following her as she walked towards Jessie and Sue. He looked like an excited child who was dying to tell her something.

"Let me see," Julia whispered, prying Jessie's fingers off her sore hand. "You didn't have to do that."

"I did," Jessie said. "Are you angry with me?"

Julia smiled. She didn't want to let Jessie know that she had been right about it being highly satisfying to watch Jerrad be punched in the face. If it were anyone else, she wouldn't have condoned the violence, but she hoped Jessie might have knocked some sense into the deranged man.

"I'm not angry with you," Julia said softly as she rested the ice against Jessie's bright red hand. "I think we need to take you up to the hospital."

"Julia?" her father mumbled.

"Just a second," Julia said as she wiped the tears from Jessie's cheeks. "I feel like the appropriate thing to say right now would be not to do it again."

"Or just not to tuck your thumb in when you punch somebody," Sue suggested as she blew on her still wet nails. "But also, what Julia said. *Naughty!*"

"You're going to make an ace mum," Jessie said, before glancing at Julia. "Must run in the family."

Julia rested her hand against her chest, her heart swelling at the sentiment. Looking into the young

Espresso and Evil

girl's eyes, it put everything into perspective. She didn't need her café to feel complete, it was just a nice extra to have. She glanced at Barker on the village green as the police officers handcuffed Jerrad and not Barker. She might not have done things the same way as her sister, but she had created a life for herself, despite having thought she had wasted her years with the man being dragged towards the police car.

"Julia?" Brian muttered again, his hand dragging over his chin as he glanced from her to the wall behind her.

"What?" she snapped, not wanting to leave the special moment.

"The painting," he said, glancing behind her again. "I think I've found it."

"*How?*" Sue cried, jumping up, careful not to touch her nails.

Instead of saying anything, their father nodded at the wall he was staring at. They turned around together, their mouths opening when their eyes landed on the giant landscape painting in the gold frame on the wall among the stock photography.

"Are you sure?" Julia asked. "I thought it was a print."

"It's a Murphy Jones," Brian said with so much

certainty, Julia felt like he had just muttered a name she should have heard of, but hadn't. "And that's one of his pre-war landscapes from when he lived in Peridale briefly in the early 1900s. They're rare to come by, and the last time one was discovered, it sold at auction for well over a million."

Sue gasped, her hand clasping over her mouth, the money making her completely forget about her nail polish. Julia stared at the dull, dreary painting. She took a step forward, the thick brush strokes jumping out at her.

"Anthony is a clever swine," Brian mumbled, sounding a little impressed. "He hid it in plain sight. Most people wouldn't know a Murphy Jones if it hit them in the face, especially his early work."

Julia crept forward, her eyes honing in on the missing screw on the left side of the painting.

"*The screw!*" she cried, lifting her foot up and clasping her sole.

"I beg your pardon?" Sue exclaimed.

"I stepped on a screw the night we found Anthony," Julia said, glancing back to the counter where she had stepped on the sharp object. "They were trying to steal the painting, but something interrupted them."

"Your café alarm," Jessie mumbled, still

Espresso and Evil

clutching the ice to her hand. "It spooked them."

"They've been waiting until the scent died down so they could come back for it," Julia said with a nod as she stared at Sue's red nail polish. "Jessie, do you still have that picture of the sugar on your phone."

Jessie nodded and pulled her phone out of her jeans, wincing as she did. Julia unlocked it and opened the gallery. She was surprised to see that the most recent picture was a selfie of Jessie and Billy smiling up at the camera. Julia suppressed a little grin as her heart fluttered. She glanced at Jessie who didn't seem to remember the picture was there. Julia flicked through to the picture of the sugar sachets. She zoomed in on the blurry red writing, and then at Sue's nails.

"I know who killed Anthony Kennedy," she whispered as she pocketed Jessie's phone. "Sue, take Jessie to the hospital. Dad, you're coming with me."

Thankfully for Julia, nobody argued. She hurried back over to her own café, quickly flipped the sign from '*OPEN*' to '*CLOSED*', before jumping into her father's car.

"How did you know the painting was in the café?" Julia asked as they sped across the village.

"I didn't," he said with a knowing smile. "That part was by accident. But I remembered why I knew the name Edwards. Oh, Julia, you're not going to believe this one."

CHAPTER 14

For the third time that day, Julia found herself at Rosemary Kennedy's cottage. When they pulled up outside, the van was gone and the front door was closed. She peered through the window into the sitting room. Gareth was sitting on the couch, a laptop on his knee.

"How do we get inside?" Julia asked. "We can't just knock on the door after turning up earlier and then leaving."

"Why not?" her dad asked, already getting out of the car. "It's not like we don't know them."

Julia scratched at her legs, remembering the nettle stings from earlier in the day. The sun was starting to wane in the sky, but the long summer night was far from over. She hoped to have put an end to the whole sorry affair by the time the sun drifted past the horizon.

Giving up on trying to think of an excuse, and half wishing she had had the foresight to bake a cake to bring if only to have something to hold, she got out of the car and followed her father down the garden path.

He pressed the doorbell and her heart pounded in her chest. She wondered if she had pieced things together correctly, knowing that if she hadn't, she was about to embarrass herself. She thought back to the painting in Happy Bean, still not able to believe it had been sitting under everyone's noses the whole time.

Gareth answered the door, his laptop in his hands. He barely looked up from it as he grunted. Julia guessed he was asking what they wanted and why they were there. Living with Jessie had given her plenty of practise translating *'teenager'* to *'adult*

Espresso and Evil

English'.

"Is your mother home?" Brian asked, his voiced commanding authority.

"No," he said, snapping his laptop shut and looking up at them. "She's gone out with Barb."

Julia and her father glanced awkwardly at each other, but to their surprise, Gareth doubled back into the cottage leaving the door open. Not wanting to question the invitation, they stepped inside, closing the door behind them.

They followed Gareth through to the kitchen, where Yelena was slicing a loaf of tiger bread into small slices. She looked up and smiled before continuing with her work. Gareth put his laptop on the counter and yanked open the fridge. He grabbed a carton of orange juice and drank directly from the spout. Julia inhaled deeply, stopping herself from correcting him like she would Jessie.

"I don't know when they're coming back," Gareth said as he wiped his mouth. "Could be ages."

"They've gone to get food," Yelena said with a sweet smile. "Barb is cooking as a thank you to Rosemary."

Gareth looked at the nurse out of the corner of his eyes before tossing the carton into the fridge. He scooped up his laptop and walked through to the conservatory, sitting in one of the wicker chairs so that he was just in view.

"He looks just like his father," Brian whispered as they stared around the blindingly white and clean kitchen. "Got his attitude too."

"He's not so bad," Yelena said, glancing at the conservatory. "Hormones. I remember my son at that age."

"You have a son?" Julia asked, not knowing why the information surprised her.

"Two back in Ukraine," Yelena said with a nod. "They are with my mother."

She pulled her phone from her pocket and flicked to a picture of a teenager with his arm around a toddler, both with dark hair like their mother. They were beaming up at the camera with pure and innocent smiles.

"They're beautiful," Julia said, ignoring the usual pang she got whenever she saw a young baby. "You must miss them."

"I send money home. I do this for them."

Julia nodded her understanding as Yelena resumed slicing the bread. When she was done, she looked through the cupboards until she found the one with the plates. She scooped up the slices and displayed them neatly in the middle of the kitchen

Espresso and Evil

island.

Much to Julia's relief, the front door opened and Rosemary and Barb returned with shopping bags. They walked into the kitchen, both of them staring curiously at Julia and Brian, although they appeared to be trying their best to hide it behind smiles.

"I think I left my phone here," Brian said quickly before tapping his empty pocket. "Have you seen it?"

"I don't think so," Rosemary said as she put the bags on the counter. "I can have a look around if you like?"

Brian patted down his jacket, rolling his eyes and laughing as he pulled his phone from his inside pocket.

"What am I like?" he asked, blushing a little as he glanced at Julia. "I must be getting old."

Barb climbed up onto one of the stools at the island, her long hair back in the signature bun it had been in when Julia had first met her. She exhaled heavily and rested her head against her hand. It looked like she had endured a long and stressful day.

"Did you get everything moved okay?" Julia asked.

"I wouldn't recommend that company, let's just say that," Barb said through pursed lips. "Wouldn't know how to be gentle if they tried. You'd think I wasn't paying them."

"Can I invite you to stay for dinner?" Rosemary asked airily, making it more than obvious she wanted them to refuse and was just trying to be polite.

"Yes," Brian said quickly before Julia could answer. "That would be lovely. Thanks, Rosemary. It'll give us a real chance to catch up."

Julia tried her best to smile, but she looked at her father and widened her eyes. He gave her a look that read *'just go along with it'*, so she didn't question him, she just hoped he knew what he was doing.

***

JULIA ATE HER DINNER OF BEEF casserole uneasily, wondering if it was possible to taste arsenic in food. She used more bread than she usually would, hoping it would soak up the poison if it had been slipped in while cooking.

"What made you want to work at Happy Bean?" Julia asked Gareth when they had finished eating at the kitchen island and were now sipping their drinks in awkward silence. "I thought you were at college?"

Gareth shrugged, glancing awkwardly at his

Espresso and Evil

mother. She smiled across the table as she tucked her neat grey curls behind her ears before sipping her wine, not taking her eyes away from her son.

"Money," Gareth mumbled with a shrug.

"Anthony didn't leave us a lot," Rosemary explained. "He wasn't the best businessman when it came down to it."

There was a murmur of agreement, which explained to Julia why Anthony's murderer was so desperate to get their hands on the painting.

"Does Jack still own the antiques barn?" Brian asked Rosemary after sipping his wine.

"He died last year. His son has taken it over now," Rosemary said, almost glad for the change of subject. "I have no idea what he'll do with it. I was almost relieved when Anthony told me he was opening a coffee shop, if only to get out of the antique business."

"It's not so bad," Brian said.

"Well, it turns out what he got into was a lot worse," Rosemary said, glancing at Gareth again. "He made sure to tear as many lives apart as he could before he died."

"Like Timothy Edwards," Julia said casually. "It's a shame he had to die too."

There was an uncomfortable shuffle around the

table. As though Julia had just dropped a conversational bomb, Rosemary and Yelena stood up at the same time picking up their plates.

"I'll do it," Barb said, standing up and grabbing the plate from Yelena. "It's only fair I pull my weight if you're going to be putting me up here."

Rosemary passed her plate around to Barb and sat down again. She stared blankly at Julia as she tossed back the rest of her wine.

"Gareth, why don't you go and clean up the living room so we can go through?" Rosemary asked, glancing at Barb as she washed up the plates as Yelena passed them to her.

Gareth huffed and slid off his stool. He pulled his phone out of his pocket and walked through to the living room. Julia looked through the conservatory as the sun started to slowly edge closer to the horizon, making the dim spotlights under the counter and above the island struggle to keep up.

"I heard your boyfriend hit Jerrad," Rosemary said. "His nose is broken."

"Does that upset you?" Julia asked.

"I'm sorry?" Rosemary replied, recoiling her head a little. "What do you mean?"

"Well, Jerrad is now your boyfriend, isn't he?" Julia asked. "Or is it not that serious?"

Espresso and Evil

Rosemary lifted her glass up to her lips, but it was empty. She looked at the equally empty bottle of white wine in the middle of the table before sliding off the stool, appearing to be avoiding Julia's stare at all costs.

"I'll grab another one from the cellar," she said as she walked over to a door, which she quickly slipped through.

"Can you grab my pills, Yelena?" Barb ordered. "They're upstairs on my bed."

Yelena nodded and slinked out of the kitchen, disappearing down the dark hallway. The sound of the TV drifted in from the living room, but the prickly silence in the kitchen was impossible to ignore. Brian sipped his wine as he quickly looked at Julia with a small nod.

Julia slid off her stool and gathered up the rest of the plates. She took them over to the sink and placed them with the others as Barb washed them, her painted fingernails bobbing in and out of the bubbles.

"That's a pretty colour," Julia remarked as she leaned against the counter. "What's that shade called?"

"Blood Rose," Barb replied with a polite smile as she grabbed the next plate. "She has a dishwasher, but I prefer to keep my hands busy."

"I find dishwashers don't get things quite clean," Julia said. "Blood Rose. That's an interesting name. It almost looks like blood, doesn't it?"

Barb looked up at Julia, a slight arch appearing in her brow, lining her wrinkled skin.

"It's one of Yelena's," Barb said with a shrug. "It's one of those long-lasting ones."

"Still keeps its shine though."

"I suppose it does."

"Almost like real blood," Julia said as she pulled Jessie's phone from her pocket. "That's what I thought this was."

She pinched the screen and zoomed in on the red writing on the sugar before showing it to Barb. She glanced at the picture, but a reaction didn't register on her face.

"What's that?" she asked as she looked down at the water.

"Just a little something somebody knocked up to frame me for Anthony's murder," Julia said as she slotted the phone away. "Arsenic poisoning is quite a nasty way to kill somebody, don't you think?"

"I haven't given it much thought."

"Are you sure?" Julia asked, folding her arms across her chest as she leaned into Barb's ear. "I

Espresso and Evil

think the problem is, you gave it far too much thought, at least every Friday when Anthony visited you at Oakwood Nursing Home."

"Excuse me?" Barb cried with an awkward laugh as the plate slipped from her hands and into the water. "What are you talking about, you silly woman?"

"A lot of people don't know that you can slowly poison somebody with arsenic," Julia said. "I didn't know that. Did you know that, Dad?"

"I didn't," he called across from his seat at the island.

"The funny thing about arsenic is that it can stay in your system and wreak havoc. A little bit can get in your bones, and stay there. It can kill a person quite slowly if left undetected, but if you're being given a drop in your coffee, let's say, every Friday, it can be quite dangerous. Of course, you knew that, didn't you Barb? That's why you poisoned your son."

Barb pulled her hands out of the sink, her eyes trained on Julia. She grabbed the tea towel and wiped the suds off her fingers, before tossing it onto the island.

"I've heard quite *enough* of this!" Barb snapped. "Your mother was a fantasist too."

Julia gulped hard at the mention of her mother. She glanced at her father, his gaze giving her the strength she needed.

"Oakwood Nursing Home is rather expensive, isn't it?" Julia asked. "That's why you plotted to kill your son when you found out about the painting. Was the pension fund running out a little quicker than you expected, or did you not think you'd live this long?"

Shaking her head, Barb walked across the kitchen, but she stopped in her tracks and turned to face Julia.

"You have no idea what you're talking about," Barb said. "You're just a silly little baker with ideas above her station."

"That's funny because you're not the first person to say that," Julia said, walking forward so that she was face to face with Barb in the dim light. "Would I be right in guessing you heard that from your son? The son who visited you every Friday out of guilt. He might have been a conman, but you were still his mother, even if it was a flying visit. What was it? Ten minutes a week? He sipped his coffee, told you what he was up to, and left?"

"He checked his watch the whole time," Barb said bitterly, echoing what she had said at the

Espresso and Evil

nursing home. "Babbled on about antiques even though he knew I didn't care. His father was in antiques too, and just as useless at it as he was."

"Except the day he slipped into the conversation that he had acquired a rare Murphy Jones painting, I bet your ears pricked up for the first time in years. I suppose he didn't think you'd know who he was. I'd never heard of him. Why would I have? But he was quite famous, or so my father says."

"For people of a *certain* generation," Brian said with a firm nod. "They used to teach about him at school."

"You knew all about Murphy Jones, and his days before the war, painting the Peridale landscape," Julia said, tapping her finger against her chin. "You knew *at least* enough to know those paintings were valuable."

Barb's jaw clenched as she stared ahead at Julia, her face becoming nothing more than a shadow as the sun drifted past the horizon.

"The fool was stupid enough to tell me exactly where he'd hidden the painting," Barb scoffed darkly. "Thought he was clever."

"This painting has caused quite a storm in a teacup," Julia said with a sigh. "Everybody wanted to get their hands on it. Rosemary, my ex-husband,

Agatha Frost

even Gareth perhaps, you all thought you were entitled to a slice of the money, but only *you* knew where it was, so you slipped arsenic into your son's coffee once a week, and you waited. You watched and waited until he died, so you could slip in and steal the painting. You even managed to get one of the screws out, but you were startled. Somebody broke into my café, and the alarm scared you off. You fled, and you've been waiting ever since to go back and take it, knowing that nobody had a clue it was there. They might not have noticed it was even missing."

Barb laughed coldly and shook her head. Her bony hands drifted up to her hair, which she checked to make sure was all still in the bun.

"My son underestimated you," Barb said with a sigh. "It's almost a shame nobody will believe you against a little, frail, old woman."

"They might believe me though," Rosemary said, her voice echoing around the stairway down to the cellar as she slipped out of the shadow. "Did you really kill my husband for the sake of keeping your room at the nursing home?"

Barb turned around and faced her widowed daughter-in-law. Julia almost expected Barb to put on her forgetful old lady routine and try to wriggle

Espresso and Evil

out of things, but her steely expression didn't falter.

"They've been threatening to evict me for weeks," Barb snapped. "They want *thousands* a month! I gave birth to the boy!"

"It doesn't give you the right to kill him," Rosemary said, her voice cracking with sadness for the first time since her husband's death. "I might not have liked the man, but that's low, even for you, Barb."

"I would have shared the money!" Barb cried desperately. "We *deserved* it. It's not too late, Rosemary. The painting is still there. We can *deal* with this!"

"Like you dealt with Timothy Edwards?" Julia called out, forcing Barb to spin around again. "I suppose he was somewhat surprised to see you turn up at his flat. You didn't have time to poison him slowly, so you did it in one go. I watched the man die."

"I'd known about their seedy affair for years," Barb whispered. "He was just *one* of them. When he mentioned that he'd bought the painting from Timothy, I realised it was only a matter of time before he realised the true value."

"You killed him to keep him quiet."

"He was *nobody*!" Barb cried. "He was just one

of Anthony's playthings!"

"He *loved* your son," Julia said, the anger bubbling in her voice. "He loved Anthony more than any of you did, and you punished him for that. Were you going to go after Maggie next? I'm sure you wondered if there was a chance he had told her too."

A flash of amusement flashed across Barb's thin lips before she turned on her heels and ran for the door. Another figure appeared from the shadows, stopping her dead in her tracks.

"How could a mother murder her own son?" Yelena mumbled as she held Barb in place after dropping the bottle of pills to the ground with a clatter. "You're a monster."

"I've been *good* to you!" Barb cried. "I brought you with me! Let go of me, you *stupid* girl!"

Tears lined Yelena's eyes, but she didn't let go of Barb's shoulders. In the distance, the piercing screech of police sirens shot through the air.

"Just in time!" Julia announced, clapping her hands together. "Thanks, Dad."

Brian waved the phone, winking warmly at her. Barb looked around the room before she began thrashing against her nurse, but it was in vain. Yelena was a mother, and she understood what it

Espresso and Evil

actually felt like to love her son.

Seconds later, the police burst through into the house, shouting and waving their flashlights as they did. Barb was in handcuffs in an instant despite her struggling. Yelena collapsed into the wall and began to sob.

"Julia?" Barker's voice called down the hallway. "I got your dad's text. Are you okay?"

"We're fine," Julia said as he burst into the kitchen, pushing past the officers as they dragged Barb down the hallway. "Thanks for coming."

"Why wouldn't I come?" Barker asked, pulling Julia in and squeezing her tight to his body. "Oh, Julia. I was so worried. Why do you put yourself in these situations?"

"Because it's the right thing to do," she whispered. "And I should have done right by you and told you the truth when I had the chance."

"I don't care about that," he whispered, hooking her chin up to kiss her. "I don't care about any of that. I love you."

***

JULIA RETURNED TO HER EMPTY HOME after giving her statement, but only momentarily.

Agatha Frost

She grabbed what she wanted, fed Mowgli, and it wasn't long before she was back at Rosemary's cottage.

Once she had given her statement, Rosemary shuffled into the kitchen and collapsed into a seat. She grabbed the bottle of wine she had brought up from the cellar, and instead of pouring it into a glass, she drank from the bottle.

"I always hated her," Rosemary said, wincing through the alcohol. "I think she always hated me too. All of that nicey-nicey stuff earlier was just because she had nowhere to go. I never even suspected she knew about the painting."

"But *you* did," Julia said, letting Rosemary know she knew about the lie earlier in the day. "You're not perfect in all of this, Rosemary. The second you found out about your husband's painting, it consumed you too. Did Jerrad bring it up?"

"It was all he talked about," Rosemary said with a sigh. "I don't know how you were ever married to the fool, Julia. He's incessant."

"You were using each other for information, but the ironic thing was neither of you actually knew anything," Julia said with a soft smile through the dark. "Is that why you forced Gareth to take a job at the coffee shop?"

Espresso and Evil

"I thought Jerrad had to slip up eventually if he found out where the painting was."

"And he thought the same of you," Julia said with a sigh. "Two wrongs don't make a right."

"I'm done with him," Rosemary said after taking another swig of the wine. "It was nice dating a younger man, but they have nothing to talk about. I'm going to focus on my son and me from now on, and if I find another man, he will be somebody who loves me for me. I thought Anthony did once, but I was young and blind. There have been people like Maggie and Timothy since the start of our marriage. I even thought your father was in on the action too, but he loved your mother too much for that. You and your sister are too hard on him, you know that?"

Julia suddenly felt guilty. She thought about the boys on Yelena's phone, and then about the little boy in Katie's stomach. She owed it to that baby to unite her family so he didn't grow up in the same situation she had.

"I know," she said. "Am I okay to use the bathroom?"

Rosemary nodded and wafted a finger towards the staircase in the hallway. Julia crept up the stairs, but instead of going to the bathroom, she opened and closed all of the doors until she found the one containing Yelena.

"I never even got to sleep here," she said. "It's nicer than the room at Oakwood."

"You know you can't stay here," Julia said.

"I know," Yelena said, looking up at Julia with a soft smile. "Why didn't you tell them?"

Julia laughed softly as she sat next to Yelena. She picked the woman's hand up and nodded to the photo frame on the nightstand, the only thing she had unpacked.

"When I figured out the writing on the sugar packets was your nail polish and not blood, I knew Barb hadn't acted alone. My sister painted her nails red, and it reminded me that I'd seen you painting Barb's nails the same colour. She might have been cunning, but there was no way she could have darted across the village like the person I saw on the security footage. You broke into my café, and you tried to frame me, but I suspect it was only on Barb's request."

"She said she didn't know how her son died," Yelena said, glancing at the sweet boys in the picture. "She said we were framing you to cover our tracks, just to be safe. I was going to send my part of the money to Ukraine. She said if I didn't help her, she'd have me fired from the nursing home. I didn't

Espresso and Evil

have any choice coming here with her. She was broke. She wasn't even paying me to be her personal nurse, I was just scared of what she would do if I didn't come."

"I know," Julia said, reaching into her handbag to pull out the rolled up stack of red notes. "This will be enough for a flight home, and hopefully some for you to start a new life. It's only five hundred pounds, but it's all I have."

"I cannot take this," Yelena said, holding up her hands and shaking her head.

"Somebody gave it to me to help, and I was ungrateful, so now I'm passing it on to somebody who it can *really* help," Julia said, forcing the money into the nurse's hands and closing her fingers around it. "I'll be fine. I always am."

Yelena looked down at the money and smiled as a tear tumbled down her cheek. She didn't say anything, instead pulling Julia into a tight hug. When the women finally parted, Julia wished her luck and slipped back downstairs, where Rosemary was with Gareth in the sitting room.

"I'm so sorry," Rosemary said as she hugged her son. "I let money blind me, just like your father. You can stay at catering college and live your life for you. I love you."

Gareth mumbled something before pulling away and shuffling out of the room and up to his bedroom. Rosemary and Julia smiled at each other, both of them understanding the complexities of teenagers.

"Does that mean you're staying in Peridale?" Julia asked, leaning in the doorframe.

"I owe it to my son," she said, looking up at the ceiling. "I always wanted children, but I thought I had left it too late. I went along with Anthony because he didn't want anything weighing him down. I was forty-eight when I fell pregnant. It was a miracle. Doctors called me a *'geriatric'* mother! *Ha*! They said I was a *'rare'* case, and the chances of me carrying him full term weren't great. Having Gareth made me believe in something bigger and better. I should have plucked up the courage when he was a baby to leave Anthony, but it was all I ever knew."

"Some men have a habit of making us think there's nothing better out there," Julia said, knowing that feeling all too well. "But trust me, there is, and you deserve it."

Rosemary smiled her thanks as Julia backed out of the sitting room. She walked towards the front door feeling lighter and freer than she had in weeks. When she walked out into the dark, her heart

Espresso and Evil

fluttered when she spotted Barker's car.

"Can I offer the lady a lift?" he called through the open window with a soft smile from ear to ear.

Without a second thought, Julia climbed into the car and kissed Barker. Her past might have been in the village having his nose plastered up, but her future was right in front of her. She deserved to be happy, but so did Barker, and she was never going to jeopardise that ever again.

CHAPTER 15

The next morning in the café, things seemed to go back to normal. Happy Bean was closed and her café was full again with all of the regular faces. It turned out more than a couple of people had their own stories to share about Barb, and even though Julia didn't care for the gossip, she was glad they were doing it in her café once again.

"This is *impossible*!" Jessie cried as she attempted

Espresso and Evil

to hold a wooden spoon with her arm encased in a cast from elbow to fingers. "I feel like the tin man."

"But you look like the scarecrow," Dom exclaimed. "Please will you let me put highlights in your hair?"

"No," Jessie snapped.

"They'll bring out your eyes," Dolly added.

"My eyes are fine where they are," Jessie said with a roll of her eyes.

Julia shuffled past them and grabbed the fresh chocolate cake she had baked that morning from the fridge. She knew it might only be temporary that her café was busy, but she wasn't going to miss what could be one of her last chances to feed the villagers her baked creations.

She headed back into the café, pleased to see Barker walking in on his lunch break.

"Is that chocolate cake?" Barker asked with wide eyes. "My favourite!"

"Baked it especially," Julia said, glancing at the clock, glad that Barker had come in just on time. "One slice or two?"

"Two, please," he said after leaning across the counter to peck her on the cheek. "I've missed your baking."

Julia sliced two generous chunks out of the cake

before placing it in the display case between a plate of éclairs and red velvet cupcakes. She quickly made Barker an Americano and placed them in front of him on the table nearest to the counter.

"Barb is singing like a canary," Barker mumbled through a mouthful of cake, chocolate cream on his chin. "Full confession. Turns out she got the arsenic from a resident at Oakwood who bragged about having some left over from the Second World War! It was totally expired, which explains why it took so long to kill Anthony, but still lethal."

"Has she mentioned Yelena?"

"Who?" Barker asked.

"Nobody," Julia said, containing her smile. "I suppose the old woman had some compassion left in her after all."

While Barker finished the first slice, Sue and Dot walked into the café, followed quickly by her father and Katie. She was glad they were all on time.

"What's *she* doing here?" Sue mumbled out of the corner of her mouth as she glanced at Katie's large bump. "Is this a stitch-up?"

"No, it's a truce," Julia said, waving a small white handkerchief in the air. "A fresh start for the sake of the limes in your stomachs."

"Actually, mine is the size of a banana!" Katie

Espresso and Evil

squeaked proudly.

Sue shook her head and scowled in her direction, which Katie seemed to take offence to as she looked the other way, her arms folding under her enhanced bosom.

"What Julia is trying to say is, you need to get along for the sake of our family," Brian said, stepping between the two women as he rested a hand on each of their shoulders. "Because like it or not, we *are* a family."

"Does that include me?" Dot mumbled through a mouthful of the second slice of chocolate cake she had swiped from Barker's plate.

"Yes, it does, Gran," Julia said. "And Barker, and Jessie. We all need to be there for these babies, so they grow up in the most loving environment possible."

Sue and Katie both sighed before glancing at each other. Julia nodded to Sue, who reluctantly held a hand out in front of her father. Katie meekly accepted the hand, sending half a smile to Sue.

"Is that it?" Julia asked. "I didn't believe that."

"I'm not *hugging* her!" Sue exclaimed. "I don't know if what she has is catching."

"This is why I didn't want to come, Brian!" Katie cried, stamping her high-heels into the floor.

Agatha Frost

"*She* is jealous!"

"Oh, for the love of chocolate cake," Dot cried, spitting crumbs everywhere. "I hate to say it, but Julia is right. It's not about you, it's about the babies."

Sue and Katie looked guiltily at the floor, and then at each other, their eyes lingering a little longer this time.

"Sorry," Sue mumbled.

"Yeah, me too," Katie replied.

"Wasn't too hard, was it?" Brian said, pulling them both into his side for a reluctant hug.

"This is good cake," Dot said as she licked the chocolate from her fingers. "I thought your baking had dipped over the last couple of weeks, but who could blame you considering the situation. It's back on top form though!"

"I'm surprised you're not upset you have nothing to protest," Julia said as she took the empty plate and put it on the counter. "Mr Shufflebottom is going to miss having you blackmailing him for t-shirts."

"Well," Dot said, standing up and unbuttoning her blue cardigan. "I went for *one* last trip."

She ripped open the cardigan, and a gasp came from everybody, except for Sue. Julia read the words

Espresso and Evil

over and over again until they sank in.

"*I'm going to be a great-great-grandmother to twins!*" Barker read aloud from the t-shirt.

"I tried to tell you yesterday before Jessie decided to play *Grand Theft Auto* in the village," Sue said as reached into her pocket to pull out a tiny black and white scan picture. "It turns out there are two limes."

Katie let out a horrified squeak before turning on her heels and stomping out of the café. Brian shrugged his apology.

"I should go after her," he said as he pulled Sue into a hug. "Congratulations. I'm so happy for you, my little girl."

"Thanks," Sue mumbled, her cheeks burning.

"Oh, I almost forget to mention," he said as he headed to the door. "I spoke to Jack's son and he's agreed to let me take over the antique barn. I'm going back to what I know best. I realised I couldn't bring a child into this world and not teach him the value of work."

"That's great news," Julia said, happy to know her father would be in the village more often. "See you later."

"Bye, girls."

Julia and Sue turned to each other with a smile.

Agatha Frost

It felt like a small victory, but it was like they both knew they had their father back.

"*Twins?*" Julia said, a smile beaming from ear to ear. "You're having twins!"

"*Surprise!*" Sue mumbled, her cheeks blushing.

Julia pulled her into a hug. She could feel her sister's nerves at the thought of having to give birth to two babies, but Julia couldn't contain her excitement.

"Babies are like buses," Dot exclaimed as she looked down at her t-shirt. "One doesn't come for ages, and then you have two at once."

After having a cup of tea, Sue and Dot left the café, leaving Julia and Barker alone. She sat across from him, but she instantly jumped up when Jerrad walked into the café, with two black eyes and a plastic support over his nose.

"I come in peace," he mumbled, his voice nasally and muffled. "*She's* not around, is she?"

"Jessie is in the kitchen," Julia said, resting a hand on Barker's shoulder. "What do you want?"

Jerrad walked carefully into the café, looking around as though he was about to step on a land mine. He stopped in his tracks a couple of metres away from their table, and stuffed his hands into his pockets.

Espresso and Evil

"I came to apologise," Jerrad said meekly. "I'm sorry."

"You're what?"

"Sorry."

"I heard that. It's just I've never heard you apologise before."

"Neither have I, and I think it might be the painkillers they've got me on, but for now I mean it." Jerrad paused and gently patted the structure holding his nose together. "She's got a mean right hook, I'll give her that."

Julia didn't say anything. Even though Barker had taken the blame for the punch and escaped charge free, Jerrad could have told the police the truth about what had happened, but he hadn't. Julia had spent the entire night expecting police to come knocking on her door to take Jessie away for assault.

"Well, I appreciate that," Julia said, still not wanting to be nice to him. "Anything else?"

"There is actually," he said, reaching into his inside pocket to pull out a folded manila envelope. "I got my lawyer to make another copy. Same terms as before, but I thought we could both sign them together so we know there's no backing out."

"Divorce papers?" Julia asked, her mouth drying as he pulled the thick wad of white paper out of the envelope.

"Unless you've had second thoughts?" he asked with a playful smirk as he handed the pen to Julia.

Julia snatched the pen out of his hand and scribbled her signature faster than she had ever signed for something before. She watched carefully as Jerrad signed next to her name, making sure that he was using the right hand and it was his real signature. She was surprised when he didn't pull any tricks.

"I'll get these to my lawyer," he said as he tucked them into his pocket. "It'll take a while for it to be official, but you'll know when it happens."

"Thank you," Julia said, nodding at him. "I really mean it."

Jerrad smiled and glanced down at the floor. She noticed a pale white line on his finger where the wedding ring had been.

"Now we can both move on," Jerrad said. "For real, this time."

"What will you do next?"

"Go back to the city," he said, glancing over his shoulder at the coffee shop. "Why did I think I could run a coffee shop? I've spoken to Rosemary, and she said she's going to keep it and turn it into something else, so you don't have to worry."

Espresso and Evil

It took all of Julia's power not to breathe a huge sigh of relief. The floor beneath her suddenly felt a lot firmer, and it had never felt so good.

"Well, good luck," Julia said.

"You too. Who knows, maybe I'll run into that painting on my way out? Wouldn't that be a nice stroke of luck?"

"Maybe," Julia said through a strained smile.

"Look after her, Barker," Jerrad said, turning on his heels and heading for the door. "She's a good woman, I just realised it far too late."

Jerrad left the café, leaving them both in a stunned silence. Barker reached up and squeezed Julia's hand, letting her know everything really was fine.

"Maybe I should have told him the painting was a fake," Julia said.

"*What?*"

"That's why my father turned up yesterday," Julia said with a knowing grin. "Timothy Edwards' grandfather was Martin Edwards, an infamous art forger. The painting was nothing more than an elaborate copy, and anybody with a million pounds to spend on a Murphy Jones painting would have known that. It turns out that Anthony Kennedy really was a terrible antiques dealer."

"So, all of this was for nothing?" Barker exclaimed with a stunted laugh. "He died for nothing? Have you told any of them?"

"No," Julia said. "I think it's better they all live with the shame of what that painting did to them. Might stop them from doing something stupid again."

Barker's eyes twinkled up at her for a moment before he started laughing.

"You're brilliant," Barker said as he stood up. "I hope you know that."

"You're not so bad yourself, are you?" Julia asked. "There was no stolen gnome, smashed window, or hanging basket, was there? You were investigating Anthony's murder, even if you weren't on the case. That's why you turned up at Rosemary's cottage, the nursing home, and Timothy's flat."

"Nothing gets past you," Barker said as he fastened up his jacket. "I couldn't sit back and do nothing while your name was being dragged through the mud. As usual, you were always two steps ahead of me."

Julia knew that Barker truly was a good man. Even though he had barely been able to speak to her or look at her, he had still gone out of his way to help her. She knew that's what true love was.

Espresso and Evil

He left the café, so Julia walked into the kitchen, where Dolly and Dom were drawing pictures in flour on the work surface, their tongues poking out of their mouths.

"Where's Jessie?" Julia asked.

They both nodded to the back door, neither of them looking up from the masterpieces they were creating. Julia walked across the kitchen and pulled on the heavy door that opened onto the tiny yard behind her café.

Standing between the bins and the gate were Jessie and Billy, sharing their first kiss. Biting her lip, Julia retreated back into the kitchen without making a sound. It was a moment she wasn't going to interrupt.

"What's she doing?" Dom asked.

"She's been out there for ages," Dolly added.

"Nothing," Julia said, trying her best to conceal her beam. "Wash your hands. Let's bake something!"

If you enjoyed *Espresso and Evil*, why not sign up to Agatha Frost's **free** newsletter at **AgathaFrost.com** to hear about brand new releases!

Coming July 2017! Julia and friends are back for another Peridale Café Mystery case in *Macarons and Mayhem!*

50521281R00160

Made in the USA
San Bernardino, CA
25 June 2017